Witchwild

Emma
Fischel

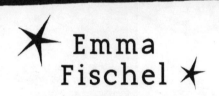

nosy
crow

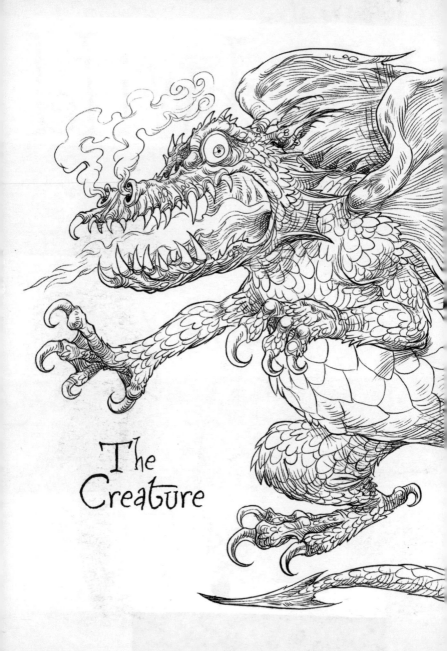

The
Creature

Flo

Mum

Hetty

Ghoul

Forest Pixie

Troll

First published 2016 by Nosy Crow Ltd
The Crow's Nest, 10a Lant Street
London SE1 1QR
www.nosycrow.com

ISBN: 978 0 85763 498 6

Nosy Crow and associated logos are trademarks
and/or registered trademarks of Nosy Crow Ltd

Text © Emma Fischel 2016
Cover and inside illustrations © Chris Riddell 2016

The right of Emma Fischel to be identified as the author has been asserted.

A CIP catalogue record for this book is available from the British Library.

Printed and bound in the UK by Clays Ltd, St Ives Plc.
Typeset by Tiger Media.

Papers used by Nosy Crow are made from wood grown in
sustainable forests.

1 3 5 7 9 8 6 4 2

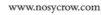

www.nosycrow.com

For Anna of the seven-league sandals.
Witchhiker beyond compare…

x

A NOTE TO ALL WITCHKIDS

Rumours have been whizzing round my school. Rumours that there's ANOTHER globe in the sky with kids living on it – but NOT witchkids like us.

Those kids can't spin webs from their fingers. Smoke never streams out of their ears when they're cross. They don't have forest pixies, or unicorns, or go swimming with merboys. And not ONE of their trees can talk.

It sounds a dull sort of globe to me. And I think all you witchkids – from the Shiverlands, the Narrowlands, or wherever – will agree that we're lucky to live where we do.

BUT...

There is a problem with living on a witchglobe so stuffed full of magic. And it's this: If we don't look after it properly, things can go wrong. VERY wrong.

As I discovered when I was stuck out there on the Wild Isle.

There's a word in Fangwegian for the terror I felt on that Wild Isle. It's ponkenfunkflittonstromp. Which means terror the size of a MOUNTAIN.

That's how the terror felt to me. HUGE. Much too big for a witchkid to handle.

But I DID handle it. So here's my advice, witchkids. If you ever have a moment of ponkenfunkflittonstromp, be as brave as you can. And NEVER give up.

Because one thing I learned is this: No matter how bad things get – there is always HOPE.

And one last bit of advice, witchkids. Keep watch. At ALL TIMES. Watch out for creatures with glowing green eyes. And if you ever spot one – run.

Then HIDE.

Florence Skritchett

Part
One

Chapter 1

I'm Florence Skritchett – known as Flo – and I live in Haggspit, the capital of South Witchenland. And the morning this story starts I woke early. *Very* early.

I opened my eyes – and straight off, I got goosebumps.

Good goosebumps. THRILLING goosebumps. Because today was Monday, the last week of term.

And then ... it was *Witchen Week*!

I jumped out of my bed – a high bunk bed – and hopped on to the whoosher, hovering right next to it. And I went whooshing round and round my room, as fast as I could.

Witchen Week...

I felt SO excited I could hardly breathe. The best holiday of the year – and it was *almost* here.

And if Witchen Week was almost here, then so was *Witchen Day* – the second Saturday of Witchen Week, the best day of the WHOLE YEAR for us Witchenlands witchkids.

A day of fun and food and presents. A bit like Fangfest is for you witchkids in the Narrowlands, or Stroggenbonk for you witchkids in the Shiverlands.

I did one last whoosh around the room, then whooshed myself down and into my den.

It's a cosy space, my den. Underneath my bunk bed, with a long squishy seat, and a desk – and my big board of pictures at one end. Pictures that mean a lot to me.

I curled up on the seat, hugging my knees tight, and stared at my pictures. Pictures of Skritchetts. Pictures of Witchen Week – all taken at Kronebay.

Kronebay...

Just thinking about Kronebay made the goosebumps grow bigger. My FAVOURITE place in the whole of Witchworld. Only five days to go, then we'd *be* there. In Kronebay, in my holiday home – Vistarikka Villa.

I hugged my knees tighter and stared at my Witchen

Week pictures. Some taken inside Vistarikka Villa. Some out in the garden. Some down on the beach.

Skritchetts fishing for spriggles in the rock pools. Racing a shoal of baby sea serpents in the shallows. Diving off the rocks with mermaids...

And Dad, LOTS of pictures of Dad.

Me and Dad.

Me and Dad giving a concert out in the garden – Dad on the glinkle, me on the firkelhorn. Me and Dad on the cliff top – me looking at a tiny chirruppella perched on Dad's hand.

Me and Dad, on Witchen Day evening. Standing in the sitting room. Both staring at the twinkling lights of the Witchen tree, Dad's arm round my shoulder.

Dad...

My *missing* dad.

I saw Dad go missing. Saw it actually happen – more than two years, eight months ago – up in the far north of Witchenwild. Saw Dad struggling to fight off a huge ghoul. Struggling to save *me*...

And Dad DID save me. But not himself.

Because he got trapped. Dad, the ghoul – they both got trapped. Hooked to a gigantic rocket by the ghoul's huge claws.

Then the rocket went screeching right up into

the sky. And exploded. Shattered into tiny pieces, right over the Ice Volcano.

We had no idea if Dad survived, not for two whole years. But now we have proof he did. *Proof.*

I stared at my pictures. At Dad, my missing dad – then I heard shrieks. Loud shrieks. Excited shrieks.

The shrieks of a witchteen…

Hetty, my sister.

It was ASTONISHING. Not the shrieking itself – because shrieking is something Hetty does a *lot*. Especially when her friends are around.

No. It was the shrieking happening this *early*.

Because Hetty does not DO early. Hetty says being a witchteen is busy and important work – and mainly done at night. And that witchteens need sleep in the morning.

But not today. Today Hetty was awake, and I could hear her feet pounding across her bedroom and out into the corridor. Then—

BAM!

Hetty pushed my bedroom door open and burst in.

Hetty's hair was sticking out, sideways and up. She had smudgy black stuff smeared round her eyes – but her actual eyes were shiny and bright.

"Flo," she shrieked. "FLO! It has *happened*! At LAST!"

She turned sideways, and pointed at her nose. "There!" she shrieked. "There, Flo! A *bump*. Look. LOOK!"

Oh. The nose...

Hetty's nose is small and neat and straight – and she despises it. She spends AT LEAST two hours every day checking it. Longing and *longing* for a truly witchy nose. One with lots of lovely big lumps and bumps. Because most of her friends are starting to get bumps – but not Hetty.

Until today.

"It's not a *big* bump," said Hetty. "But it's a start, Flo. A START!"

I looked.

And there *was* a bump. But a VERY tiny one...

Hetty flung herself down in my den, next to me. "Flo, Flo!" she said. "Now Errken will almost *definitely* be my boyfriend. My ACTUAL boyfriend! Probably TODAY!"

Errken – Errken Padlokk. A witchboy who Hetty is trying *very* hard to make her boyfriend.

"Good things are about to happen, Flo," Hetty said, beaming and nodding. "I know it. I *know* it! My nose is a SIGN!"

Then she grabbed my hands. "Mum," she said. "I'm showing Mum next. And Grandma! Everyone! ALL Skritchetts must see my bump!"

Then her mouth turned right down, her head drooped, and – oh no – Hetty started wailing. "Why is Dad not here?" she wailed. "WHY? Where *is* he?"

Hetty's mood changes VERY fast. Now she was wailing so loud my ears began to hurt.

"If ONLY Dad were here to see it!" she wailed. "Dad is missing out on SO many important milestones. ALL my important milestones. Dad doesn't even know I nearly have a boyfriend. He doesn't know about the bump! And Dad SHOULD know!"

And then – oh no – Hetty started wailing more.

"I don't know what to *think*!" she wailed. "One minute I think he'll be back very SOON. The next I wonder if he will EVER be back. And I don't *like* it! It is not GOOD for a witchteen to feel this *confused*!"

Then her head dropped right down. "I want Dad back," she wailed. "NOW! NOOOOOOOOOOOOOOOOOW!"

"Hetty," I said. "Dad *will* be back. He WILL. And soon. I can just FEEL it."

Because I can. I keep getting this feeling. A

tingling, thrilling goosebumpy sort of feeling. Like something good is going to happen.

And Dad – he will be back. I know he will.

I just KNOW.

Chapter 2

Kika and Lily – Kika Rorrit-Mogg and Lily Jaggwort, my two best friends – were waiting for me on the corner that morning. Both beaming.

Lily stepped forward as soon as she saw me. "Flo," she said, "we have a surprise for you. Because of Saturday. Missing Kika's party."

I did miss it – because, on Friday night, me and Mum had a Lakktarnian. It's Mum's favourite takeaway, and mine too. Small sharing dishes, and spicy. But not so spicy it makes my eyes water, like a Farflung does.

But there must have been something wrong with

the Lakktarnian. Because me and Mum were both ill that night, and most of the next day. So I had to miss Kika's party.

And now Kika started nodding wisely at me. I knew why. Kika was about to quote the Book.

Kika is always quoting the Book – *Two Hundred Utterly Important Things a Witchgirl Should Know.*

She did now.

"Because Flo," she said, "a lovely way to show a friend you CARE is to surprise them with a gorgeous gift or terrific treat."

Lily nodded. "So that's what me and Kika are doing," she said, getting a parcel out of her school bag. "Surprising you. With this."

She looked at the parcel thoughtfully. "It's not actually MY idea of a gorgeous gift," she said, handing it to me. "But we hope it's yours."

It was.

I opened it upstairs on Skybus 401, all of us squashed on to the back seat.

"A snow troll globe!" I said. "Thanks!"

Then I shook it, and watched little flakes of snow fall gently in the globe, settling on the snow trolls – three furry white trolls, antlers gleaming and sparkling.

"Is it the sort of gorgeous gift you like?" Kika said

anxiously. "Is it?"

"It is," I said. "It really is."

Snow trolls… The snow trolls singing…

The *proof* that Dad had survived.

Because Hetty had been camping near the Ice Volcano, near where the snow trolls live. And she heard the snow trolls singing. But not singing the song of the snow trolls, that strange but beautiful tune snow trolls usually sing.

No.

These snow trolls were singing a different song. A different tune. A *special* tune…

A tune me and Dad had made up. A tune only Skritchetts know. And there was only one Skritchett who could have taught it to them…

Dad.

And, as Skybus 401 swung left and down towards the school stop, I clutched the globe in my hand. Shook it once more – and stared.

✦

"Emerald Class," said Mr Prankett, bounding into the classroom. "Good morning."

He beamed round the room. "Who can tell me why we celebrate Witchen Week?" he said.

Loads of witchkid hands shot up in the air. Mr Prankett pointed. "Henka," he said. "Henka Sprigg."

"Because of the olden days," Henka said. "When all Witchenlands witches did skrumpel seed planting."

"Correct!" said Mr Prankett.

All us Witchenlands witchkids know about skrumpel seed planting.

How the city witches – whole families, even tiny witchkids – would head off to join the country witches. Bedding down in tents in the fields, and in their sheds and outbuildings.

How, between them – from Monday to Friday – all those city and country witches planted the skrumpel seeds in long straight rows.

How those tiny skrumpel seeds grew – in only three months – into huge tall trees, groaning with skrumpel fruit. Fruit that was picked to feed those olden days witches throughout the long cold winter.

And how, inside every one of those picked skrumpels was a seed, ready for next year's planting. Because – no witches know how or why – each year, when the first flakes of snow flutter down on to the skrumpel trees, they VANISH.

Skrumpel seed planting doesn't happen like that now, of course. Not since witches came up with intelligent magic machines. But we still celebrate the skrumpel seed planting with Witchen Week.

Mr Prankett beamed even brighter. "I am sure

you do NOT need me to tell you that this is the last week of term," he said. "Which means some terrific treats. Starting right now!"

He looked round the classroom. "Because this morning in witchglobe studies, Emerald Class," he said, "we are going to see a special screening. *Skyhunter* – the witchflik!"

Skyhunter, the witchflik! I felt thrilled.

Skyhunter is my absolute favourite. It stars Destiny Daggett – a fearless witchkid, who roams the witchglobe fighting crime and dodging deadly peril.

Up to now, *Skyhunter* has only been on the witchscreen, so us witchkids watch it at home. But now, with the first-ever *Skyhunter* witchflik, we could watch Destiny on a skyscreen. A *huge* skyscreen.

And we were getting to see it today. TODAY! Four days early.

Even Lily and Kika – who think they are a bit too old for Destiny Daggett – were looking thrilled. But NOT Mamie Swip. Mamie Swip's hand shot up.

Mamie's mother is Education Minister, part of the government. She makes lots of rules about what witchkids should and shouldn't do in school – and Mamie knows every single one of them.

"Mr Prankett," Mamie said sternly. "Terrific treats are for the very end of term. Which this is not. Not until Friday."

And she hadn't finished. "Another thing, Mr Prankett," she said. "Going to a *Skyhunter* witchflik is NOT witchglobe studies."

"Mamie, there you are wrong," said Mr Prankett. "What is the purpose of witchglobe studies?"

"To teach witchchildren about the astonishing witchglobe they live on, and the ways of the witches who live on it," said Mamie.

"And this *Skyhunter* witchflik—" said Mr Prankett. But he didn't get any further because there was a loud clattering then the door flew open. And standing there, flushing a very dark green, all out of breath as if he'd been running – was Mervikk.

Mervikk Ashbok.

Late *again*.

Mervikk keeps being late, especially these last few weeks.

Mervikk stood there, his hair all on end. He looked a mess. There was a smudge of something on his left cheek. His backpack was half-buckled. His robes were buttoned on all the wrong buttons.

"Sorry, Mr P," Mervikk said. "Sorry. Sorry. SORRY. I did try to be on time. I just missed my

skybus. I got to the skybus stop and there it was –
GONE! Way up on Skyway 1."

Mervikk flung his arm out to point at an
imaginary Skyway 1. Only his arm knocked Henka,
who sits at the table right by the door, and her specs
went flying.

"Oops," Mervikk said, picking the specs up and
handing them back to her. "Sorry, Henka. And sorry
again, Mr P. Sorry."

"Better late than never, Mervikk," Mr Prankett
said, as Mervikk turned, took one step towards his
desk – then tripped.

"Sorry, Mr P," Mervikk said, sprawled out on the
floor. "Sorry, sorry. Forgot to do my laces up."

Mr Prankett got out his spellstick, and pointed it
at Mervikk. "*Abrakkida Rune*," he said.

Mervikk shot off the floor and flew through the
air, across the classroom. And, as he flew, his laces
did themselves up, his robe rebuttoned itself, a
damp cloth appeared out of nowhere and wiped
the smudge off his face, and a hairbrush sorted out
his hair.

"Thanks, Mr P," said Mervikk, grinning as he
landed in his chair, at my table. "Sorry again."

"Mervikk, you are welcome," said Mr Prankett

But I could see a small frown on his face. Not a

cross sort of frown. A thoughtful sort of frown, as if he was wondering something. But I had no idea what.

Chapter 3

Screen 10 of Haggspit Skyscreen was full of witchkids. Not just from Charms – my school – but from Cults and Cacklings and lots of other lower schools around Haggspit.

Then the lights went dim, and music started. Scary music. Low, menacing notes. Just two notes, starting slow and quiet, then getting faster and faster, louder and louder. And, up on the skyscreen, huge green letters appeared...

FROM THE MAKERS OF SKYHUNTER COMES...

TERROR IN THE FLATCALMS
A DESTINY DAGGETT ADVENTURE!

The letters slowly faded away. Then the sea began to appear. Underwater – as if we were seeing it through the eyes of some big BIG creature, swimming faster and faster…

Then whoosh – we were out of the water, and on the deck of a big searider. And Destiny Daggett's first skyscreen adventure began.

It was twenty action-packed minutes straight off. Destiny Daggett up against a vicious gang of smugglerwitches. All chases, stunts and explosions.

Then, just as Destiny got captured by the smugglerwitches and it all looked over for her – there was an even deadlier peril…

A sea serpent.

But NOT the usual sort of sea serpent. Not those gentle giants of the sea – big as a double-decker skybus. Those sea serpents who swim about eating tiny planty things all day long. Causing no harm to witches.

No. *This* sea serpent was mean and nasty. A rampaging, terrifying sea serpent. All because it lived in the Flatcalms.

We did the Flatcalms in witchglobe studies this

term. It's where three seas meet – the Southern Sea, the Serpent Sea and the Deepwaters. It's a huge island of rubbish, almost the size of a small colony like Witchenfinn – bobbing about in the sea.

It's because of the currents that so much rubbish ends up there. All sorts of rubbish. Old rusting imms – intelligent magic machines of all kinds – and potion jars, spellsticks, skychatters, skyrider numberplates… It all piles up in the Flatcalms.

In the *Skyhunter* witchflik, that big island of rubbish was leaching magic into the water. And all that leached magic POISONED the sea serpent. Turned that big gentle giant into a vicious attacking machine.

A *mutant*.

It started attacking the searider. Picking off the smugglerwitches one by one. Until there were only two witches left on board…

Two witchkids. A cabin boy – and Destiny Daggett.

They teamed up, fought off the mutant time and again. Then they finally got rid of it in one dramatic explosion.

I enjoyed every minute of it…

Unlike Mervikk.

★

Me and Mervikk are partners on school trips and he sat next to me, frowning, on the schoolshuttle as we flew back to school. Not jiggling, not fidgeting like he usually does – but frowning and still.

Which meant Mervikk was thinking. Thinking very, very HARD.

I waited.

I had no idea what Mervikk was thinking – but I knew I'd find out. Because most of the thinking that goes on in Mervikk's head comes out through his mouth.

It did now.

"That writer got it ALL wrong," Mervikk said, in a grumbling sort of voice. "That sea serpent was a *boring* mutant. Not a CONVINCING mutant. Hardly a mutant at all. Just swimming about, being a mean and vicious version of itself."

Mervikk frowned more. He was NOT happy. "And that sea serpent didn't *change*," he grumbled. "And it *should* have changed. Should have grown five times its size. Or sprouted big lumps and bumps and spikes and tusks. Been DIFFERENT."

His shoulders slumped. "And *another* thing, there was no TRIGGER for the sea serpent."

I gaped at Mervikk – which I quite often do. "Trigger?" I said.

"Something that set it off, made it go mutant," Mervikk said. "Because a PROPER mutant, a convincing mutant, would just be a *normal* sea serpent most of the time. Then the trigger happens – getting hurt, getting hot, whatever. And when the trigger happens, THAT'S when it goes mutant."

Now both Mervikk's eyebrows were knotted together. "Besides, that writer got it wrong," he said crossly, "because a mutant sea serpent – it's not LIKELY, is it?"

"It's a witchflik, Mervikk," I said. "A story. It doesn't *have* to be likely. I mean – we all know that a bit of rubbish in the Flatcalms would NOT cause a mutant."

Mervikk stared at me, looking baffled. "No, no, no," he said. "I don't mean the *story* wasn't likely. I mean the *sea serpent* wasn't likely."

Now it was my turn to be baffled. I gaped again. "Explain…" I said.

So Mervikk did. "All that magic leaching into the sea," he said, "it wouldn't be a BIG fish who went mutant. It would be one of the tiddlers. A sprikkelfinn, say. That tiny body, that big dose of magic – it would affect a sprikkelfinn *way* quicker."

Now Mervikk started nodding. "That writer

24

should have made it a little sprikkelfinn who went mutant," he said. "So the sprikkelfinn could be swimming around, being totally normal and then – bam! – the trigger, whatever it is, happens. And the sprikkelfinn could grow. Get HUGE. Sprout horns and bulges and other stuff. Become a big vicious ugly sprikkelfinn mutant."

He paused. Looked at me proudly. "And *that*," he said, "would be more dramatically effective."

"Dramatically effective?" I said, more baffled than ever.

Mervikk nodded. "More of a SHOCK, " he said. "Something small changing into something big – all because of a trigger. My sprikkelfinn would be a WAY more interesting mutant than a *sea serpent*."

Then Mervikk started frowning again. "But would a sprikkelfinn be the best mutant?" he said. "What about a larbinspike? Would that be a more dramatically effective mutant? A little larbinspike that grows into a gigantic *mutant* larbinspike?"

Mervikk spent ALL DAY trying to decide what small sea creature would be a better, more dramatically effective mutant than a sea serpent.

I tell you, I was glad to get home.

But when I got home, the witchhailer started flashing.

Chapter 4

"FLO," Grandma's voice boomed out over the witchhailer. "FLO! FLO? FLOOOO? IS THAT YOU, BACK FROM SCHOOL? ARE YOU THERE?"

"I am, Grandma," I said. "And you don't need to shout, I can hear you quite clearly."

Grandma has her own little house, right at the bottom of my back garden. It's cosy and snug, and painted pale green – and Mum calls it an annexe.

Grandma doesn't. Grandma calls it a shed.

Grandma is always grumbling about her shed. Grumbling at Mum for banishing her to a shed.

Grumbling that Mum is a cruel and ungrateful daughter.

Grumbling that her shed is pokey and lonely.

Grandma is lying. She *loves* her shed – it's just she loves grumbling at Mum even more.

And the witchhailer is new. A link between Grandma and us.

Mum got it put in after last week. Because last week, Grandma was brewing up a potion in her kitchen. She went to get a jar of goblins' eyelashes from her larder – but she tripped over one of her frogs hopping across the floor.

She flung out her arm to try and stop her fall – but it got wedged in the frog flap in her back door. She lay there – totally stuck – for over TWO HOURS before Mum found her.

So Mum got the witchhailer put in, and now Grandma wears a special bracelet, black and chunky, with a green button she can press that lets her talk to us.

And even though Mum has told her ten times – *at least* – that she doesn't have to shout, she still does it…

Like now.

"COME DOWN TO THE SHED, FLO!" Grandma bellowed. "HURRY! HURRY! HURRY!

I HAVE *SPOTTED* IT!"

I ran. FAST. Down the garden, and in through Grandma's front door.

Grandma was jumping up and down in front of her magic mirror, dressed – as usual – in old black robes and a pointy witchy hat. Looking like something from my witchhistory book.

Her magic mirror was stretched out all along one wall. Showing one big picture – of cliffs and coves, and a lagoon.

Grandma jabbed a finger at the picture. "There, Flo," she said. "There! That's where it is. Look. Look! You can just see it. Behind that rock."

I looked. I could see it. A paw. A HUGE paw. Bright yellow and bristly, with four sharp claws on the end...

Yes! I knew what it was straight away.

The Trigoggladron...

A creature from a book, *Magical Myths of the Witchenlands*. A book of myths that turned out to be TRUE.

And me and Grandma have been trying to find the Trigoggladron for MONTHS.

Because the Trigoggladron is a three-headed ogre that knows *everything*. And the Trigoggladron will answer any three questions a witchkid asks it...

Which meant I could ask it where Dad was.

✳

"Flo, let us *go!*" said Grandma, hitching up her robes and rushing towards the back porch.

I rushed behind her.

Grandma has a broomstick stand in her back porch. It's got five broomsticks in it – and the smallest one is mine.

Grandma gave it to me. She's been teaching me broomstick riding, and now I'm quite confident. So I jumped on, pressed my knees against its sides, and took off.

And, yes – I know it's against the law for under-sixteens to ride broomsticks. But I think that's a silly law. ALL witchkids should have the chance to ride a broomstick. It's fun.

(The witches in charge of this book would like to make clear that they in no way encourage this DANGEROUS MAGICAL ACTIVITY. And that any witchchild who rides a broomstick undertakes it at their own risk.)

Today was windy – the windiest day I have EVER been flying. The wind was blowing my hair all over my face, and the gusts kept knocking my broomstick sideways as we went lurching and bucketing about in the sky.

Then, just outside Klink, there it was – Lugubrikk Lagoon, spread out below us. The wind whipping up choppy grey waves all across it…

I saw the paw straight away. Poking out from a pile of boulders – big BIG boulders, lumpy and grey and as tall as my house.

Then we landed.

"Ready, Flo?" whispered Grandma, right in my ear. She opened the basket on her broomstick, and got out a cake.

"Glimbel cake," she whispered. "Three different fillings! Delicious!"

She handed it to me. "Remember," she whispered. "First, feed the hungry head with cake. Next, soothe the grumpy head with your finest singing. And then – ask the head of all knowledge your question."

Now Grandma wagged a finger in my face. "But ask your question carefully, with cunning, with GUILE. It is not enough to ask where Lyle Skritchett is. For – who knows? – perhaps there is *another* Lyle Skritchett somewhere in Witchworld. So your question must be clear. 'Where is Lyle Skritchett, witchscreen presenter, champion harpy hurdler, ghoul slayer, and father of Henrietta and

Florence Skritchett?' *That* is what you must ask."

Grandma's eyes shone. "And then," she whispered, "we shall have our answer! We shall discover where your father is. At last!"

And she beamed at me.

I tried to beam back...

I couldn't.

That paw was HUGE. And *very* bristly. And it belonged to an ogre. An ogre with not just one head, not just two – but *three*.

And I have already met one of the creatures from *Magical Myths of the Witchenlands* – the Haggfiend – who was truly terrifying...

But now Grandma was creeping towards the boulders. Creeping round the side. Creeping towards the paw.

I followed, trembling.

But...

Oh.

There was no ogre. No huge three-headed creature, snoring and dribbling.

Just a huge nest. A nest as big and round as my garden pond. A scrappy, messy nest. With things strewn around it. Bits of rubbish. Shiny things. Trinkets...

And leaning out of one side. Poking out the side

of the nest, round the side of the boulders.

The huge bristling paw from a Trigoggladron costume.

Grandma picked up the huge paw and stood there, glaring down at it. "A costume?" she hissed. "All this effort – all for a COSTUME?"

Something inside me lurched. Relief first, that there was no Trigoggladron. Then sadness. Because that chance of finding out where Dad was – it was gone.

Then I looked harder. At the nest … the size, the shape, all the collecting. And I realised what it was. Something I saw on *Wild and Wonderful Witchglobe*.

The nest of a FLITTERSWIPE…

"Grandma," I said. "We need to go."

Too late. We heard a squawk behind us. And there it was. Long neck stretched out. Big beak snapping open and shut – a VERY indignant flitterswipe.

It started hissing. Staring at the huge paw Grandma was holding in her hand.

Oh no. It thought Grandma was stealing from its nest.

It started flapping its wings. Stamping its webbed feet. Getting ready to charge.

"Flo," said Grandma, dropping the paw and backing away. "I think it is time we left."

And, as the flitterswipe charged, we turned and ran.

Chapter 5

Mum saw the scratches straight away – as soon as I walked in through the back door. Because the flitterswipe managed quite a few pecks at me, and at Grandma, before our broomsticks outflew it.

Mum came rushing over. "Flo!" she said. "You have scratches. Scratches! On your face, your arms! What from? Why?"

"Kristabel," said Grandma. "Flo and I were forced to FLEE."

"To flee?" said Mum, panicking. "Why were you fleeing? What were you fleeing from?"

"From a VICIOUS ATTACK, Kristabel," said

Grandma. "By a flitterswipe!"

"A flitterswipe?" gasped Mum. "Where? *Where?*"

"At Lugubrikk Lagoon," said Grandma.

Now Mum stared at Grandma. "And *why* were you at Lugubrikk Lagoon with Flo?" she said. "WHY EXACTLY?"

Then her eyes narrowed. "I hope this was not one of your *Outings*," she said.

Because Grandma has a history of taking me on Outings – Outings that Mum does NOT consider suitable for a witchkid.

"Kristabel," said Grandma proudly. "Flo and I were indeed on an Outing. We were on a MISSION."

Mum's eyes got even narrower. "A *mission*?" she said, staring at my scratches. "What kind of mission?"

"A mission to find the Trigoggladron!" said Grandma.

Mum's mouth dropped open. She glared at Grandma. Small puffs of smoke started coming out of her ears. "You took Flo on a mission to find the Trigoggladron?" she hissed, between clenched teeth.

"I did," said Grandma. "I spotted its paw in my magic mirror – or at least what *seemed* to be its paw. Poking out from behind a big boulder. Naturally Flo and I swung into action!"

"Swung into action?" said Mum, grinding her

teeth now.

"Indeed," said Grandma proudly. "All this time I have been searching," she said. "Searching United Witchenlands. But that wretched creature is so *very* difficult to track. Always on the move. Vanishing, then reappearing somewhere quite different. And finally – TODAY! – I thought I had found it. That this was Flo's chance to ask it some questions."

Mum started screeching. "You took Flo – *my daughter!*" she screeched, "to find the TRIGOGGLADRON? An *ogre* – with three heads?"

Mum slumped down on a breakfast-bar stool, pressed her hand to her forehead and went palest green. Then she started groaning.

"Kristabel, stop being such a fusspot," said Grandma, eyes popping. "I have absolutely no idea why you are making all those silly groaning noises. Flo is perfectly all right."

Mum jumped off the bar stool and stomped over to Grandma. "You will NOT take my daughter to find the Trigoggladron," she hissed, right in Grandma's face. "Not EVER again. Promise me. *Promise!*"

Grandma's eyes started popping more. But just then a huge thunderclap boomed out, the back door flew open – and a parcel shot into the kitchen and landed on the worktop…

A thunderbolt delivery for Mum. The brand-new issue of *Scoop!*

✦

Mum is the boss of a magazine, *Hocus Pocus*. And its biggest rival is *Scoop!*

A new issue of *Scoop!* arriving by thunderbolt delivery means Miranda – who works for Mum – thinks Mum needs to see it immediately.

And that, usually, is NOT good news.

It wasn't.

Mum stared down at the cover, all thought of the Trigoggladron gone. "Look at that," she hissed. "LOOK AT THAT!"

I looked.

A whole lot of witchcelebs were on the front cover, all wearing black tops with white writing on them…

I CARE!

And in big bold letters above the whole thing it said this…

READERS – JOIN OUR CAMPAIGN

There was more on the cover. A big box on the right-hand side, with pictures of three little witchkids, and another headline…

WITCHKID CARERS –
THE SHOCKING TRUTH REVEALED!

"Look, look!" hissed Mum, flicking through the pages. "*Scoop!* is campaigning. Doing good works. Being CARING and CONCERNED!"

Then Mum's skychatter rang again. She snatched it up. "Yes, Miranda," she said. "It has arrived… Yes, indeed, Miranda. I agree. I *agree*. We too must campaign. But for what? What?"

Then she swirled off into her office and slammed the door.

I pulled up a bar stool and stared down at *Scoop!* Opened it up. Started reading all about the '**I CARE!**' campaign.

How it began when a *Scoop!* reader wrote in. She told *Scoop!* about how she was ill. And how her daughter, Romilla, looked after her.

How Romilla was only eight years old. But she got up at five every morning to get herself ready for school. Then she got her younger brother and sister up, and fed, and ready.

How Romilla did all the cooking and cleaning. And all the shopping too – including a copy of *Scoop!* every week for her sick mum.

The reader asked if *Scoop!* could organise a fun day out for Romilla. To say thank you for all the things she did.

And that got *Scoop!* thinking. Setting up the **I CARE!** campaign. To give days out and holidays to witchkid carers all over United Witchenlands.

Then *Scoop!* talked to lots of witchkid carers. Asked them how they felt. And wrote down what they said...

"I love my mum and I want to look after her. But it makes me sad that I can't go to Shreeken Park after school and play with my friends." Klemm, aged 10

"My legs get tired from shopping and cleaning, so I don't run fast, and other witchkids never pick me for their gripball team." Imboll, aged 8

"When I get up at night to look after Mum, I muddle things in school the next day. And then I have to stay in at playtime." Doran, aged 9

"I feel different from other witchkids, but I want to feel the same." Monikka, aged 12

"Once, two years ago, a witchlady looked after my mum all day and I went to the zoo. I was happy because I got to feed bananas to the Lakktarnian skringotts. I'd like to feed them again, but I don't know where the witchlady lives." Oskar, aged 8

Then I turned the page, and saw this:

HURRY! HURRY! HURRY!

HELP 100 WITCHKID CARERS HAVE A HOLIDAY
THIS WITCHEN WEEK!!!

Chapter 6

Scoop! had a big plan for Witchen Week.

A way to kickstart the **I CARE!** campaign right now. To give 100 witchkid carers the Witchen Week break they deserved.

Because *Scoop!* had found out that lots of witchkid carers get no real break in Witchen Week. No holiday. No fun. How they still had to cook and clean and care.

And that was *Scoop!*'s big plan. To pay for replacement carers, so the witchkids could have the week off.

They were being helped by top businesswitch,

Aggratikka Thropistikkan. She was giving them money. And space in her office, and staff, to help sort holiday places for the witchkids.

I sat there, thinking. Staring at *Scoop!* and what it said…

ACT NOW!
Invite a witchkid carer to join YOUR Witchen Week holiday!
Click HERE to fill in the form, and show YOU CARE!

Then I heard the *putt putt putt* of Hetty's skyscooter, landing in the back garden. And Hetty's feet going *clack clack clack* towards the back door.

She flung the door open. Stood there, eyes shining, hands clasped. "Flo," she shrieked. "It has happened. At LAST – I am going on a date with Errken!"

She ran in. "Errken has asked me to MARCH beside him!" she gasped, plonking herself down in the chair next to mine. "To share a banner! A BANNER, Flo! To join the campaign!"

"And what is the campaign?" I said.

Hetty stared at me, as if I'd asked a stupid question – which I didn't actually think I had. Then she started shaking her head, and looking all impatient.

"I don't know, Flo," she said. "Some … *thingy* the government needs to do."

Then she grabbed my hands. "But THAT is not *important*, Flo," she said. "What IS important is that Errken wants me – ME! – by his side! For the campaign! To share a banner! It is a *date*, I'm SURE it is! On Thursday!"

"Hetty," I said. "About campaigns… There's one here. Will you look at it?"

Then I pushed *Scoop!* towards her.

Sometimes – just occasionally – Hetty can be almost sensible. Almost thoughtful. And she was now.

She read the whole thing in silence, eyes popping, occasionally gasping. She read all about Romilla, about the other witchkid carers…

Then she looked at me. "That is terrible," she said. "SHOCKING."

"That's what I think," I said.

✶

"Be calm, be firm. And go for it, Flo," Hetty said, standing outside Mum's workroom. "This is the RIGHT thing to do. Errken says it is important that witchteens ENGAGE with our witchglobe and the witches on it." She nodded. "And that's what your plan is doing. Engaging."

"Do you want to talk to Mum too?" I said.

"Me?" said Hetty. She cackled. "Flo. Helloooo? Witchteen with *date* to prepare for! And less than three days to prepare! So preparing starts NOW." Then she clacked off to her room.

I knocked at the door of Mum's office, then went in. Mum was standing in front of her desk, staring at her witchfixer screen.

She had the E list up on it. The Endangered section. Every single endangered species in the whole of Witchworld. She was clicking from one to the next.

"Too beaky?" she muttered as she looked. "Too hairy? Too many horns? Not cute enough?"

Then she turned. "Flo," she said. "*Hocus Pocus* needs a campaign. Perhaps a creature to save? Something cute and cuddly. But which shall it be? Which?"

And that's when I spoke. "Mum," I said. "About campaigns... Can we do the *Scoop!* one? Can we take a witchkid carer to Kronebay for Witchen Week?"

Mum's mouth dropped open. "Support the *Scoop!* campaign?" she said, looking shocked and staggering backwards into her chair. "Support a RIVAL? I can't possibly do that."

"Mum," I said, perching on the edge of her desk. "This isn't actually about *you*. It's about a witchkid. A witchkid carer who needs a break."

Mum shook her head. "No," she said. "NO."

"And it's also about us having a big holiday villa by the sea," I said. "With two spare rooms, and plenty of space. And I asked Hetty and she said yes."

Mum shook her head again. "NO," she said.

I just sat there and looked at her.

She looked back. Narrowed her eyes. "Flo," she said. "Your chin is jutting forward. Your arms are folded. And you have a *look*. A LOOK! All over your face. Take it off. I don't like that look. It's a stubborn look. Take it OFF."

"Mum," I said. "Did you actually *read* the article? Because there are witchkids out there who have to do everything for their witchmums or dads. Washing, cooking, cleaning, shopping. Witchkids as young as SIX. Witchkids who never get to play. Witchkids who have to get up at five o'clock in the morning EVERY SINGLE DAY. And before they even go to school they have to—"

Mum stuck her fingers in her ears. "Stop! STOP!" she said. "All right. We will do it. We will offer a holiday to a witchchild carer."

I beamed at her. "All we have to do is click here,"

I said, pointing.

She glared back. Then, sighing, she clicked. And the application form appeared on her witchfixer screen.

Mum sat, scowling at the form as she read. Then...

"Oh," she said. "Oh." Then she got a gleam in her eye, and a crafty sort of look on her face.

I wasn't sure what the "oh" meant. Or the gleam. Then I looked at the screen.

TICK HERE IF YOU ARE WILLING TO TAKE PART IN PUBLICITY

And underneath it said more...

Scoop! are keen to feature some of the readers who have stepped up to the Witchen Week challenge! We are looking for families to follow. Families who will show the witchpublic just how fabulous Scoop! readers are!

"Excellent!" Mum said. She beamed at me. "Flo, you are a *genius*! I can see the headline already. MAGAZINE MOGUL PUTS RIVALRY ASIDE TO HELP WITCHKIDS IN NEED."

She ticked the box. "Publicity," she beamed. "Lovely LOVELY publicity."

Then she looked at me. She looked closer.

She sighed. "Flo. It's there again," she said. "That look on your face. The chin ... the arms... All of it. And this time that look is saying you think I am WRONG."

"Mum," I said. "I want to get a witchkid carer because it's the right thing to do. Because it's *hard* being a witchkid carer. Because a holiday would be a *fun thing* for a witchkid carer. NOT because it will make you look good."

Mum's shoulders slumped. Her mouth turned down. She sighed. She drooped. "No publicity?" she said sadly. "Not even a *teeny* little bit of publicity…?"

I didn't speak. Just stared at her.

She sighed again. "Flo," she said, drooping more, "sometimes you are JUST like your father."

Then she unticked the box and started to fill in the form.

Chapter 7

That night I dreamt about Kronebay. Happy dreams. Dreams about Witchen Week. And Dad was there too, arriving at Kronebay, early one morning. Tapping on the sitting-room window, and grinning.

Then I woke up, with morning light streaming into my room. And I could *still* hear tapping.

For one moment – one BRILLIANT moment – I thought my dream was real. That Dad was there, tapping on my window.

He wasn't. But a small fluffy troll was. One paw going *tap tap tap* on the window...

Crawky.

Crawky is an urban troll – and a very brave one. One who helped me defeat the horrible Haggfiend when he was just a baby.

He's not a baby any more, but he's not very old. He's small and round and fluffy, and he loves two things: books, especially lift-the-flap books; and imms, intelligent magic machines.

Crawky *loves* imms. Domestic or industrial, roving or static – all kinds of imms. In fact, Crawky used to live in an imm. A domestic imm – an old witchwasher in the garden – before Mum got rid of it.

I opened the window and in Crawky hopped. He was clutching a book. A new one Mum bought him last week. A *Find Out About* book… *Find Out About Industrial Imms*.

We sat down in my den, then Crawky handed me the book.

I opened it up and turned to the first double page. A page full of pictures of imms. Ten of them, all big industrial ones.

"Imms are intelligent magic machines," I read. "The imms in these pictures are the biggest imms of all. They are called industrial imms. Turn the page to find out more."

Crawky pointed a paw at each of the imms, eyes shining. Then he turned the page and leaned closer to stare at the next picture – a very big imm with very big pincers.

"This is a loglugger," I read. "It is used by witches to move heavy logs from place to place. Pull the flap to see it lift a log."

Carefully and slowly, making little excited gibbering noises, Crawky pulled the flap.

"Now press the button to hear its loud engine roar," I read...

We read the whole thing. Page after page of big industrial imms – groundgrabbers, wallwalkers, brickbashers, ditchdiggers, seedsowers, potionpackers, all sorts. Crawky pressed every single button and lifted every single flap.

Then we got to his favourite page of all. A picture of a big queue of old imms right across the whole double page. And above each imm, a big heavy weight – an immobiliser...

"When imms stop working they go to special places called the Heaps," I read. "At the Heaps all the magic is taken out of them, then the imms are safe to put in the ground."

I paused.

"But first the imms must be crunched up and

made very small."

I paused again.

Crawky sat there, staring at me. One paw poised above the button. Waiting. Quivering. Desperate for me to read the last sentence…

And I did.

"Press the button to hear the big imms go CRUNCH," I read – then straight away, blocked my ears. Because the crunch is a *horrible* noise. A noise of metal being crushed by an immobiliser. A jangling grating noise. A noise that sets my teeth on edge.

But Crawky loves it.

There's just one page after that. All about TrashTax – the money businesswitches have to pay each time they take an industrial imm to the Heaps. How TrashTax helps the government to fund the Heaps. And how the bigger the imm is, the more TrashTax needs to be paid for it.

It's a boring page, though. With lots of words, but not even one picture. Crawky NEVER bothers with it – and I don't blame him.

So I left him, flipping through the book, pressing buttons and lifting flaps. And I went to have breakfast and get ready for school.

"Welcome, witchchildren," said Ms Riggle, our headteacher, "to our annual Witchcitizenship Awards!"

Witchcitizenship Awards happen every year in our school. Just before Witchen Week we have a whole school assembly and prizes are given to witchkids who have been extra good witchcitizens that year. Witchkids who do good deeds, like visiting lonely old witches to cheer them up. Or volunteering for the litter patrols around South Siren Square.

"As always," said Ms Riggle, with a smile, "we are delighted to welcome a very special guest to our assembly."

We always have a guest witch. One who speaks a bit, then hands out the awards. Last year we had Aggratikka Thropistikkan, who told us all about a charity she supported, Wild Witchglobe. A charity that campaigns for witches to look after our witchglobe better.

"Our guest today is a VERY important businesswitch," said Ms Riggle. "One who has factories across the witchglobe, including here in United Witchenlands."

Then she pointed her spellstick. "*Abrakkida Rune*," she said, and a magimirage appeared.

An image of a factory. A huge factory – full of

imms. Gleaming industrial imms. Imms grinding and mixing and squishing. Imms sifting and straining. Imms bubbling and brewing up potions.

And all over the factory, big see-through pipes – ready-potions pipes. Pipes full of gushing potions.

"But he is not here today because of his factories," said Ms Riggle. "He is here because of his GOOD WORKS. Only last year he opened, here in Haggspit – THIS!"

Then she pointed her spellstick and once more said, "*Abrakkida Rune.*"

A new magimirage appeared. A big building, with a banner strung across it…

WELCOME TO THE HURLSTRUK HAPPY HOME! GRAND OPENING TODAY!

"The first ever Hurlstruk Happy Home," said Ms Riggle. "A home to provide orphans with the same opportunities as his very own witchchildren. And a truly *fine* example of witchcitizenship in ACTION!"

Ms Riggle smiled around the assembly hall. "And now, witchchildren," she said, "please welcome Mr Potions2Go himself, Meristo Hurlstruk!"

We all starting clapping – and there he was. Strutting out of the wings. Then strutting across the stage, chest all puffed out.

He stood, staring down at us all.

"Witchchildren," he boomed. "Listen and learn! I have *empires*. I have factories, houses, islands – more riches than you can POSSIBLY imagine."

He paused. "And *how* did I get where I am today?" he boomed. "By HARD WORK! INTELLIGENCE! HONESTY!"

Now he strutted to the very front of the stage. Swivelled his eyes to stare at us all. "And witchchildren," he boomed, "should you EVER become the *enormous* global success – the powerful, respected figure – that I have become, I have three pieces of advice for you. Advice number one – STAY HUMBLE."

Well – he didn't look very humble to me. Standing there, chest all puffed up.

In fact, he looked like the yafflepeck that lives in our garden, in the woldenbore tree. It's a tiny little bird, and it struts around all day long, looking very VERY proud of being a yafflepeck. It's always puffing up its chest – just like Mr Potions2Go was doing now.

"And now for advice number two!" he boomed.

"GIVE BACK. Success is NOTHING without giving back! So give back – just as I have done with the Hurlstruk Happy Homes."

He strutted more. Boomed more. "And my FINAL piece of advice – advice number three – is *this*. CHERISH OUR WITCHGLOBE. Cherish it as I do. As all us eminent businesswitches – all us HUGE contributors to the wealth of this marvellous globe – have a duty to do."

Then he strutted over to Ms Riggle, and sat down. And we all started clapping – except Mervikk, who started whispering in my ear.

"My dad says it's his daughter who is the brains behind the Hurlstruk empire," Mervikk whispered. "The one who makes all the money. My dad says that witchman is an IDIOT. And that's why his wife just divorced him."

And, looking at Mr Potions2Go, sitting there, all smug and pompous and pleased with himself – I had a feeling Mervikk's dad could well be right.

Chapter 8

"Design a *poster*, Mr Prankett?" said Mamie Swip, on Wednesday morning. "A poster warning witchchildren about the danger of a MUTANT SEA SERPENT in Haggspit Harbour?"

"Yes, Mamie," said Mr Prankett.

Mamie narrowed her eyes. "Mr Prankett," she said, suspiciously. "Designing a poster sounds like frivolities to me – but this lesson is NOT frivolities, it is *words*. And the Class Directive for words this term is information gathering."

"This IS information gathering, Mamie," said Mr Prankett. "Witchchildren must be informed of the dangers of a mutant sea serpent. Your task is to gather the information, and convey it effectively on a poster."

Mamie was cross. "But Mr Prankett, a mutant sea serpent is *not* in Haggspit Harbour," she said. "You are asking us to convey FALSE information."

"Mamie, for the purposes of this lesson you are *imagining* there is a mutant sea serpent in Haggspit Harbour," said Mr Prankett.

Mamie's eyes narrowed more. "Imagining sounds very like creative writing to me," she said suspiciously. "Which is NOT information gathering."

Henka Sprigg's hand went up. "Mr Prankett," she said, and her voice was quavering slightly. "You don't actually think there COULD be a mutant sea serpent in Haggspit Harbour, do you? Because I am not all that happy about the thought of swimming during Witchen Week if that is the case."

"Henka," said Mr Prankett, smiling. "The sea is VAST. It is unlikely that, even if some magic does leach into it, it will affect the creatures of the deep."

Mervikk's hand shot up. "Mr P," he said, waving it about. "What about the ground? What about magic leaching into the ground?"

"That is why we have the Heaps, Mervikk," said

Mr Prankett. "To keep the ground safe."

Mervikk's hand shot up again. "But I saw an old wetdrudge just dumped the other day," he said. "In a hedge. Not at the Heaps."

"An old wetdrudge is hardly a threat to wildlife, Mervikk," said Mr Prankett. "Just as the sea can cope with the occasional abandoned imm, so can the ground."

But once more, Mervikk's hand was in the air. "Mr P," he said. "Mr P! Suppose there's a GINORMOUS pile of imms somewhere? Because some greedy businesswitch who hates paying TrashTax didn't take his imms to the Heaps – but just dumped them. Hundreds and HUNDREDS of imms! That might cause mutants! BIG ones!"

Mr Prankett smiled, but shook his head. "Hundreds and hundreds of dumped imms would be almost IMPOSSIBLE to hide, Mervikk. Sooner or later witches would find it. And there are big fines for dumping old imms. A businesswitch who did that would be ruined. Would end up in prison. So the risks are far too great."

Mervikk's shoulders slumped. He looked fed up. "Shame," he said. Then, with a sigh, he picked up his pencil, and started designing his poster.

I gaped at Mervikk's finished poster. He had done a LOT of imagining, even going on to the back…

WITCHKIDS!
BEWARE MUTANTS!

WARNING!
A mutant sea serpent has been seen in Haggspit Harbour.
But do not worry. For this is NOT a mutant to be scared of.
It is just a bit more viciouser than a normal sea serpent, and you can easily escape it.

HOWEVER – there have been sightings of OTHER MUTANTS around Haggspit.

See below for further details.

MUTANT POSSENFLOFF!
First attack in Haggspit Heights Pet Parlour!
Shop evacuated – but NOT FAST ENOUGH!
All occupants SWALLOWED WHOLE!

MUTANT ZIZZWING!
First attack in Charms school playground!
Schoolchildren in PANIC!
One witchgirl EATEN COMPLETELY, two
witchteachers HORRIBLY INJURED!

WARNING!
Most of the time mutants look **NORMAL!**
You **CANNOT** spot a mutant until it is
TRIGGERED!
A mutant may grow
ASTONISHING EXTRAS!
It may grow extra **HORNS,** for example!
It may grow to **FIFTY TIMES** its own size!

REMEMBER!
You are **NOT SAFE ANYWHERE!**
Not even in **YOUR OWN HOME!**
AVOID PAVEMENTS! BEACHES! SHOPS!
SHEDS! BATHROOMS! CELLARS!
And beware of **EVERYTHING!**
Even **YOUR OWN PET!**
And especially **TINY CREATURES!**

★

Mervikk had done drawings too. One of a normal possenfloff, and next to it, the mutant. At least ten times the size of the normal one – like a gigantic bristling ball with horns on its head, and four tusks.

And the same with the zizzwing. The mutant had huge fangs, waggling pincers, and a long bulgy tail part. Next to it, Mervikk had put a tiny dot, with an arrow pointing to it, and a label saying this was a normal-size zizzwing for scale.

"Mervikk," I said. "Those mutants… Your poster … it's not actually about the sea serpent. Hardly at all."

Mervikk gave me a huffy sort of look. "Mr Prankett told us to imagine, Flo, and I *am* imagining," he said. "In fact, I have done a lot of EXTRA imagining – so I may even get extra marks."

★

And all that imagining must have worn Mervikk out – because that afternoon we were all working quietly on a magiography wordsearch, when I heard a snorting noise beside me.

Mervikk was fast asleep. Lolling back in his chair, mouth open. Then, all of a sudden, he flung both his arms out and hurled himself sideways.

He clunked to the floor and woke up – just as Mr

Prankett ran over and helped him to his feet.

"Sorry, Mr P," Mervikk said, looking a bit dazed. "Sorry. Dreamt I was dodging a mutant possenfloff."

Mr Prankett was frowning. Probably because Mervikk has fallen asleep in class three times over the last few weeks.

"Mervikk," said Mr Prankett. "See me after school."

Oh dear. Poor Mervikk.

It looked like he was in trouble.

Chapter 9

Next morning I was eating breakfast before school when Hetty walked – no, shuffled – into the kitchen…

I gaped.

Hetty was dressed in a costume. Dressed as a snack bar, a breakfast bar. A Krunch'n'Munch bar.

She was one long orange and blue oblong with squiggly writing across it. Her arms were sticking stiffly down by her sides, and her feet were shuffling in teeny-tiny steps. She looked VERY hot and VERY uncomfortable.

"Hetty," I said. "Why are you dressed as a

Krunch'n'Munch bar?"

"Campaign," she said. But she could hardly speak. Her cheeks were squashed by the sides of the bar, and her mouth was all puckered up and pouty, like a fish.

Then one of her arms – stiffly and slowly – came up and took the head part off. "Better," she said, looking relieved. Then she tried to sit down, but she couldn't.

"Hetty, what IS your campaign?" I said, confused.

"Free breakfast bars for all witchteens," said Hetty proudly. "Because Flo – witchteens canNOT get themselves to college on time and also eat breakfast. It is a *fact*."

Hetty looked very important. "And it is today, Flo, that government spending on education is to be DECIDED. And Errken says it is our duty, as witchteens who are studying governmentals as one of their further witchsits, to ACT. To stand outside Argument House and persuade witchministers of the importance of supplying free breakfast bars to witchteens."

Hetty started looking very earnest. "At the moment, Flo, the government is planning to spend NO money on breakfast bars. And Errken says that is a DISGRACE. Do you know how many

64

witchteens fainted in our college due to lack of breakfast last year, Flo? *Seventeen!*"

Then she frowned. "Besides," she said, "it is FAIR. You teenies get a carton of kronkel-milk at playtime. And what do witchteens – who are FAR MORE important – get? Nothing!"

Then she shuffled off towards the back door and out to her skyscooter. Just as Mum swirled into the kitchen, beaming.

"Good news, Flo," she said. "We have our witchkid carer."

Then she slapped a piece of paper on the table. A print-out. A picture of a witchgirl.

"Magda Frink," Mum said. "She likes reading and playing the glinkle. She sounds an excellent match. We pick her up on Saturday morning."

The witchgirl – Magda Frink – looked just about my age. She had a big smile and orange robes, long red braids and lots of freckles.

Mum turned towards me. "One more thing," she said, with a pleading look on her face. "About publicity … could we … maybe … just do a teeny *teeny*—"

"Mum," I said. "NO."

✶

In school, we did fun quizzes all day. And I kept

hoping Mervikk would turn up – because Mervikk is a genius at quizzes and always wins prizes for our table.

In fact, Mervikk is a genius at most things. Well, except sitting still. That's how he's at Charms. Because Charms – which costs a lot – has one space a year for a genius witchkid to go free. A witchkid who doesn't have a rich mum or dad. And in our year, it's Mervikk.

So I kept hoping that maybe Mervikk was late again, that he'd arrive soon. But he didn't. Not all day.

Then the day was over, and Mr Prankett said our homework was to make a silly hat to wear tomorrow, the last day of term. So I sat in the kitchen back home, designing my hat – then I heard the *putt putt putt* of Hetty's skyscooter.

In she shuffled – sideways through the back door. She struggled and wriggled her way out of her costume, then flung herself down on a breakfast-bar stool. She looked hot and fed up.

"Veracity was there too!" she hissed. "Sharing our banner! She FAILED to understand that this was a date for me and Errken – and that Errken ONLY invited her because he is *shy*, Flo, and *cautious*. Too shy and cautious to just invite me."

Hetty slumped, elbows on the worktop. "And Veracity kept butting in, Flo," she said, "on MY conversations with Errken. And because Errken is POLITE, he had to look *interested* in what Veracity had to say — even though I know he was NOT. Because Errken is truly interested in what *I* have to say. And Veracity should KNOW that."

Now Hetty pointed her spellstick at the witchscreen. "*Abrakkida Rune*," she said grumpily, and the witchscreen flickered into life. Just as the theme tune of *Haggnews* started up.

Hetty sat forward. "We'll be on this!" she said. "Errken says so. He says our campaign will UNDOUBTEDLY be the top story!"

Errken was wrong.

"In our top story today," said the witchscreen presenter, "witches were protesting and chanting—"

"Protesting and chanting — that's us! It IS us!" shrieked Hetty, eyes shining.

It wasn't.

✦

These witches were all protesting and chanting about dragons' rights. Standing outside a ready-potions factory, all dressed as dragons — Oggentakk Browns. Waving banners demanding no more testing of ready-potions on them.

Hetty gaped. "*Dragons?*" she shrieked. "Oggentakk Browns? THAT is the top story? A protest about dragons? How can stupid old DRAGONS be more important than our campaign?"

She started chewing her fingernails. "It'll be me and Errken next," she said. "It will."

It wasn't.

"Today at Hovelhagg Palace," said the witchscreen presenter, "her Esteemed Graciouswitch, Katarinka the Second, revealed the Hovelhagg Honours List. We spoke to two top businesswitches who received medals for their services to charity."

I recognised both businesswitches. Aggratikka Thropistikkan, the businesswitch helping the *Scoop!* campaign. And Mr Potions2Go, Meristo Hurlstruk.

"Stupid old businesswitches. Stupid old MEDALS!" Hetty shrieked. "How are *medals* more important than STARVING witchteens? How? HOW?"

Once more, she slumped. "THIS will be us," she said. "This *has* to be us."

It wasn't.

"A study carried out by the Wild Witchglobe charity," said the witchscreen presenter, "reported a startling result this week…"

And it WAS startling.

Because witchboffins working for Wild Witchglobe had spent the last ten years researching the effects – if any – of magic leaching into the ground.

They set up a test site, filled it with old imms, and introduced a group of nibbets. They studied the nibbets for ten years. And this week, an astonishing discovery had been made.

One of the baby nibbets – born a few weeks ago – was VERY strange. Most of the time it looked like all the other baby nibbets. But when it felt angry, or threatened, its eyes glowed bright green. And not only that – it also *doubled* in size.

The effect lasted minutes. Until the baby nibbet calmed down. But the witchboffins were calling for VERY heavy penalties for dumping old imms. And for funding for further research into the harm that magic leaching into the ground could cause.

They were also calling the nibbet a MUTANT…

"A mutant? A mutant NIBBET?" shrieked Hetty. "What does a mutant nibbet matter when there are witcheens *fainting* in EVERY college in United Witchenlands?"

And she stomped out of the kitchen, and off to her bedroom.

But I stayed, staring at the witchscreen. At the

small hissing nibbet, at its glowing green eyes. And I felt the hairs on the back of my neck – slowly, slowly – stand up on end...

Every single one.

Chapter 10

Rumours start a LOT in my school. Rumours that go buzzing around the playground. Whispered by one witchkid to another.

They started that Friday morning. Rumours about mutants. All sorts of mutants.

Because it wasn't just me who saw the report on *Haggnews*. Lots of witchkids did. And I kept looking out for Mervikk – because Mervikk is nearly always the witchkid starting the rumours. And his rumours are excellent. But there was *still* no Mervikk.

And, maybe because it was Friday, and the last day of term… Maybe because Witchen Week was about to begin… Maybe because all us witchkids were feeling excited, wearing silly hats, playing silly games, making Witchen Day cards, eating a special Witchen Day dinner… Or maybe just because all of us missed Mervikk, and his excellent rumours…

But by dinnertime there were new rumours whizzing around Emerald Class. Rumours about mutants – and *Mervikk*.

"Did you hear about Mervikk? He got ATTACKED. A mutant gritterback!"

"I heard that! I heard that! A mutant gritterback with *seven* heads. SEVEN! Not just three!"

"It totally was NOT a gritterback. It was a zizzwing."

"Yes! A GINORMOUS zizzwing! Twenty – *thirty* – times normal zizzwing size."

"And with a waggling behind – with POISON SQUIRTERS."

"And Mervikk got four big bites on his cheek, and now he's in Upper Haggspit Medicentre. He is a medical PHENOMENON."

Mr Prankett heard the rumours. "Emerald Class," he said. "Mervikk has NOT been attacked by a mutant of any kind. And he is NOT in Upper Haggspit Medicentre."

Then Mr Prankett looked round the classroom.

72

"Mervikk is off school for very good reasons," he said. "Family reasons. And I promise you – you will see him again, straight after Witchen Week."

But I saw Mervikk much sooner than that…

I saw him the very next day.

✶

"Flo," said Mum that Saturday morning. "It is time to collect Magda Frink."

I felt excited – and a bit nervous – staring out of the skyshredder, as Mum flew us to Haggspit Heights Hall.

There was a big banner outside with writing on it…

I CARE!
JOIN OUR CAMPAIGN!

Inside, the hall was packed. One hundred witchkid carers, all standing there. All with cases packed, all looking thrilled, with shining eyes. All holding up signs with names on – of the family they were going to join for Witchen Week.

I spotted the sign first…

SKRITCHETTS

it said.

Except it was NOT Magda Frink holding it up. Not a witchkid with red braids, and freckles, and bright orange robes. No.

Because Magda Frink had bought a ticket this week – a Witchen Whirly Wheel ticket for her mum.

The Witchen Whirly Wheel is something the government is in charge of.

Millions of witches buy a ticket each week. The government takes half the ticket money to give to charities. And gives the other half as prize money.

All the tickets have seven numbers on them. And each week the winning numbers come flying out of a big spinning cauldron. A witch whose ticket matches the winning numbers gets a cash prize.

Like Magda Frink's mum.

She had a winning ticket – and it won MILLIONS. Which meant, instead of Magda, we had another witchkid carer. A last-minute replacement.

And there he was, our witchkid carer – holding up the sign, grinning and grinning and grinning at me…

Mervikk.

I was amazed. Mervikk has been in my class two whole years – ever since he moved to Haggspit.

But he has never said ONE WORD about being a witchkid carer. About his dad being ill with Stumbles. About Mervikk doing all the cooking and cleaning and shopping and nursing.

"It's not nice, Stumbles," said Mervikk, jiggling about in the back of the skyshredder as we flew along Skyway 1. "It comes and goes. Sometimes Dad gets better. Almost well again."

Then Mervikk gave a big sigh. "Trouble is, as soon as that happens, as soon as Dad's well enough to play a bit of gripball with me, the government says he's well enough to go back to work."

He sighed again and shook his head. "But Dad never IS well enough. He goes back to work – and gets worse again. So then he needs me to look after him. Like the last four weeks."

Mervikk smiled. "But not this week," he said. "NOT this week!"

He leaned forward. "Flo's-mum," he said, over her shoulder, "I have NEVER been to Kronebay. In fact – I have never been on an actual holiday. So I just want to say thank you. And I will do my VERY best to be no trouble, and to be a helpful, cheerful house guest."

"Mervikk, you are most welcome," said Mum, graciously. "And I do hope you will enjoy yourself.

We have many fun things planned for Kronebay."

Then she pressed a button on the dashboard and music – Mum's sort of music – blasted out all around the skyshredder.

"Goodbye work, hello Witchen Week!" Mum said happily, then she started singing along. Loudly.

I looked out of the window at the coast rushing by below us.

Mervikk beamed at me. "You know what, Flo," he said. "We might get lucky and find a mutant nibbet in Kronebay. OR, even luckier – there might be OTHER mutants. Bigger mutants. Scarier mutants!"

Because Mervikk had watched *Haggnews* too. And – as far as Mervikk was concerned – the mutant nibbet on the news was just the start.

Then his eyes lit up, and he grabbed my arm. "You know what, Flo?" he said. "You and me, we would make an *excellent* mutant-finding team. Because you've got the experience and—"

I had to butt in. "Experience?" I said, gaping. "Mervikk, I have NO experience of finding mutants."

"Not mutants, no," said Mervikk. "But of finding SCARY creatures, you do."

Which was true. I *did* have experience of finding scary creatures. Ghouls – who were meant to be extinct. And the Haggfiend – who was meant to be mythical.

Now Mervikk was nodding hard, beaming even more. "And luck comes in threes, Flo," he said. "So you're BOUND to get lucky again. Imagine it – first, extincts! Second, mythicals! Third, mutants!"

I gaped at him. "LUCKY? That would NOT be lucky. That would be very, very UNLUCKY!"

No. This Witchen Week – or any other week – I did NOT want to find a mutant. Not at all.

There was only one thing I wanted to find. One thing ONLY, in the whole of Witchworld.

Dad.

Part
Two

Chapter 11

"*Kronebay!*" said Mervikk, jiggling beside me in the skyshredder. "Flo, that is KRONEBAY!"

And there it was, far below us. A huge curving bay, sea sparkling and blue. Seariders bobbing about in the water. Mermaids sunning themselves on rocks. Witchkids skimming round the bay, riding bareback on two-humped peskadrons.

Thrills shivered through me. Kronebay. At last!

Now Mervikk clutched at my arm. "Which is your house, Flo?" he said. "Which one?"

"That one at the far end," I said, pointing. "The white one. Perched up high. On the sticking-out bit of cliff."

Mervikk's mouth had dropped right open. "Wow," he said. "WOW."

He stared as the house came closer and closer. All pale white wood, and two storeys tall. The pale lilac flowers of fragrant vistarikka climbing every wall that they could.

Then we landed. Right outside the front door.

"Mervikk," said Mum, turning round and beaming. "Welcome to Vistarikka Villa!"

The flexipod opened and me and Mervikk scrambled straight out. Then Mum pointed her spellstick at the house. "*Abrakkida Rune*," she said.

Straight off, things started happening. Shutters folded themselves back. Doors and windows flung themselves open. And then – the noises started. Whizzing, whirring, whining noises...

The noise of imms.

Domestic imms. LOTS of imms. All getting to work. Whizzing and whirring and whining, cleaning and tidying all the rooms.

"One rule *only* on holiday. Absolutely NO housework," said Mum happily, as bits of luggage lifted themselves out of the skyshredder and flew towards the house.

"Mervikk," Mum said, smiling at him. "You will

find your case in your bedroom. Flo will show you around. If you need me, I shall be on the south terrace."

I did *try* to show Mervikk around Vistarikka Villa. We went into the hallway. And Mervikk stood, gaping at the big staircase sweeping up the middle, and the gallery above it – but then the wetdrudge came zooming in.

And the wetdrudge kept whizzing around us, mopping and wiping, and slopping water from its bucket all over our feet as it cleaned.

So I grabbed Mervikk and we ran upstairs, and I showed him the guest room – the kids' guest room, right next to mine. And Mervikk started bouncing on the guest bed, talking about it being big and soft, and having no lumps and a sea view – then the drydrudge burst in.

It started plumping up Mervikk's pillows. Then it whizzed his rug out on to the balcony, and started beating it hard to get the dust out. And all the dust made me and Mervikk sneeze…

So we gave up, and went out into the garden.

Vistarikka Villa has a very big garden. One that rambles right around the house. With lots of steps, and bits of lawn, and an orchard, and little waterfalls, and a pond – and three terraces.

Mum was already stretched out on the south terrace. Lying on a lounger, a book open on her lap, a big yellow sunhat flopping over her face – talking to Hetty on her skychatter.

Because Hetty was still on the way. Flying along the back routes and smaller skyways with Grandma…

"See you soon, darling. Fly carefully," Mum said, putting down her skychatter.

She waved at me from her lounger. "They're just past Dribbel," she called. "Not long now."

An army of small imms were hard at work out in the garden. Mowing imms, snipping imms, shearing imms. All sorts of imms. And a little spraysquirter, whizzing around and around in the air, spraying water all over the flowers.

Then there was a beeping noise – and out came the butteldrudge. Scurrying towards Mum, carrying a big blue drink with lots of ice in it.

"Ah," Mum beamed, taking the drink. "My blorberry cordial."

The butteldrudge scurried off, beeping, to the flagpole. It started hoisting the flag – which it always does when we're at Vistarikka Villa.

It's colourful, the United Witchenlands flag. Three bright stripes across. One green, one orange, one pink. And four black stars in the corners, for the four colonies – South Witchenland, Witchenfinn, Witchenwail and Witchenwild.

The flag flapped hard, because the garden was breezy. And me and Mervikk stood there, on the terrace steps – Mervikk's head swivelling from side to side, as he stared out to sea.

"Your house is on a peninsula, Flo," he said, eyes shining. "I am staying on an actual PENINSULA!"

And it *is* a peninsula – because the cliff sticks right out, with the sea on three sides of it. Which means there is a LOT of sea to stare at – Kronebay at the front, the Sheltered Sea all round.

"Over there," Mervikk said, swivelling, and pointing. "Over five hundred miles away, that's Fangway!"

He was right. It was Klonkenprink, capital of Fangway. And I've been there four times – but not Mervikk.

"I have always, ALWAYS wanted to go to Fangway," Mervikk breathed. "And Frakkenwild. And Lakktarn. And *all* the Narrowlands. But so far I've not been to any of them."

Then he beamed at me. "Except in my head," he said. "In my head I've been to them ALL."

Now Mervikk swivelled again. Shaded his eyes, looking west. Towards a faint shadow on the horizon.

"Kraggen," said Mervikk, staring. "That's *Kraggen*! First of the Wild Isles!"

Then we heard something. Chirrupping noises. Coming from the grass…

Chirruppellas.

Chirruppellas only live around Kronebay and out on the Wild Isles. They're inquisitive little creatures. They always start chirrupping when we arrive, and hopping out to see us.

They did today.

Three, four – five little heads appeared. Five little creatures, jumping through the grass.

Mervikk crouched down. One of the chirruppellas came hopping over. Stood upright in front of him, on its strong hind legs. Shiny black eyes staring, scales glistening in the sunlight.

"They're friendly," I said, crouching down too. "Tame. Not scared of witchkids at all."

Mervikk held out his hand. The chirruppella's long flicky tongue shot out and gave his hand a lick.

"It tickles," Mervikk said, cackling.

He'd soon stop cackling. A *lot* of chirruppellas live in our garden. And they can actually be a bit of a nuisance, hopping around your feet all the time.

"It's got stumps on its back," I said. "Tiny stumps.

Little knobbly bits. Witchboffins reckon they were once wings."

Because witchboffins think chirruppellas are related to dragons.

Not the dragons us witches have now. Not the worker dragons – the Oggentakk Browns used for potion testing, or the Lumberons used for dragon-oil production. And not the domestic dragons – all the breeds witches keep as pets, like the Whiptails, and the Furnassons.

Not those dragons, no.

The *first* dragons.

The WILD dragons.

The scary ones. The dragons that used to roam Witchworld before witches domesticated them. Before witches bred them to be safe…

Chirruppellas are *much* closer relations to them.

But when chirruppellas learnt to swim, they stopped needing wings, and stopped breathing fire. They grew a long flat tail instead. Now they're fast and nimble swimmers, and they use their tail to make very quick turns in the water.

"Chirruppellas," said Mervikk thoughtfully. "They hunt nibbets…"

He looked around, a hopeful sort of look on his face. And I knew why. He was thinking about the mutant nibbet. Hoping to see one right here…

"Mervikk," I said. "One slightly mutant nibbet does NOT mean there are lots of mutant nibbets."

"Suppose not," he said, with a sigh.

And just then, we heard the *putt putt putt* of a skyscooter. And loud tuneless singing of an olden days sea shanty – "The Song of the Sirensisters".

We looked up, and there they were. Grandma and Hetty, coming in for landing.

Chapter 12

Vistarikka Villa has its own private cove. But the cliffs are so sheer, so steep, that there's only one way down to it...

A magiskelter from the back garden.

"A Helter 13!" Mervikk said, eyes shining. He hurled himself on to it and went whizzing round and round, down and down, and – far below – tumbled out on to the sand, scrabbled to his feet...

And then, he must have got straight back on again – because, here he came. Whooshing up the Helter 13, and tumbling out into the garden.

"What a ride!" he said, picking himself up,

beaming. "What a magiskelter! Way faster and smoother than a Helter 12!"

Now Grandma came stomping down the garden, carrying a bulging beach bag. "Ready!" she said, grinning her wide big gappy grin. "Me first!"

Then Grandma led the way, and all three of us whooshed down the Helter 13 and tumbled on to the sand.

Grandma got to her feet, brushed the sand off her robes, then waved her wand. "*Abrakkida Prodit, Koratikki Parvit,*" she said. "*Tugurikka, Litikka, Rune.*"

A shimmering magicreation began to appear on the sand. A small wooden hut. A beach hut.

"I shall be with you shortly," Grandma said. Then she marched inside the hut, and shut the door – just as Hetty came whooshing down the Helter 13.

I gaped.

Hetty was wearing a two-piece. A stripy top, and stripy shorts. Stripy – and VERY bright. Stripes of dazzling blue, green and orange, all twinkling and shining. With orange sunglasses, even more dazzling than the rest, covering most of her face.

She got out her spellstick. "Teenies," she said, proudly. "Watch and learn."

Then her fingers went flying. She pointed the

spellstick at the water. "*Abrakkida Rune,*" she said. And a shimmering outline began to appear.

A canoe, bobbing in the shallows – dazzling and stripy, to match Hetty's outfit, and with a bright orange paddle.

Mervikk's eyebrows shot up. He gaped at the canoe. "*You* did that," he said. "An actual magicreation! You *and* Flo's-gran!"

Hetty patted Mervikk on the head. "Spellsourcing and spellsplicing, level 4," she said. "And one day, Mervikk, you too will be capable of such spells."

Then she hopped into the canoe. "Thirty minutes' vigorous canoeing," she said, happily. "Excellent toning for the upper arms."

And off she went, paddling round the cove.

Mervikk was still gaping – and I thought he was gaping because of Hetty's spellstick skills, but he wasn't.

"How big is your sister's magic allowance?" he said. "Magicreations – they *cost*!"

Which is true, of course, whatever colony you live in. No magic supplies come free. Not anywhere.

Now Mervikk was doing the sums. "That magicreation," he said, knotting his eyebrows. "What's it using? How many units of magic energy? Two hundred zapps maybe? Every ten minutes?"

His eyebrows knotted more. "So…" he said, "in half an hour that magicreation will use *six hundred zapps* of magic energy!"

He breathed in. "Six hundred zapps," he said, like he couldn't believe it, "but … but – that's *six hexons* of magic energy! SIX WHOLE HEXONS!"

Just then, the door of Grandma's beach hut burst open. She stomped out, wearing a big black bathing suit. She had flippers on her feet, goggles over her eyes, and a snorkel in her hand.

"Who's for a swim?" she said.

"I can't swim, Flo's-gran," Mervikk said. "I don't know how."

"Can't swim, Mervikk?" said Grandma, eyes popping. "Good heavens! Then you must learn."

Now Grandma was pointing her wand at Mervikk. "*Abrakkida Mutattikk, Piskilliki Marvik, Diversikka, Optikka, Lune,*" she said. "*Neptik Non, Illik Non, Revikkto, Akwattik, Fakinikka, Strune.*"

A shower of stardust swirled out of her wand, and all around Mervikk. And then – Mervikk was gone. Transformed.

In his place was a small stumpy creature. With a sleek shiny blue coat, a big tuft of yellow hair, and a beaky sort of face.

A woddelflomp. With a VERY startled look in

its eyes.

"Off you go, Mervikk," said Grandma. "You have one hour."

But just then, behind us – I heard a shriek.

I turned.

Mum was whooshing out of the Helter 13. Glaring at Grandma, as Mervikk – the woddel-flomp-Mervikk – shuffled off down the beach as fast as he could.

"Mother!" Mum shrieked. "How could you?"

She came running towards us, pointing her spellstick. But Grandma was too quick for her. "*Abrakkida Fakerrik, Non Krustik, Non Sterrik*," she said, waving her wand. "*Offikilli, Offekilli, Devune*."

Mum's legs crumpled under her and her arms went all floppy. And the spellstick fell out of her hand…

Oh no. Poor Mum. Grandma had just done the jelly-legs spell on her.

Grandma does the jelly-legs spell – *much* too often – on me. And it is SO annoying. It makes your legs go all wobbly and floppy, then your arms, then the rest of you, including your mouth – so you end up just burbling and dribbling.

And, yes, it *is* illegal witch-harming magic. But

does Grandma care?

No.

"Mother!" Mum shrieked. And she tried to get up – but she couldn't. "Undo the jelly-legs spell. *Undo* it!"

"Kristabel," said Grandma. "I shall undo it. Once Mervikk has returned."

"But, Mother," said Mum, lying on the ground now, her mouth beginning to flop open, "we canNOT transform a witchboy in our care into a *woddelflomp*!"

"Why on earth not?" said Grandma, astonished. "Best way to learn to swim."

Then Grandma gave a big snort. "Witchkids today – mollycoddled," she said. "*All* witchchildren in my day learnt to swim as woddelflomps. Only a few casualties each year. Considered perfectly acceptable. *And*, Kristabel, you yourself learnt to swim that way."

"Yes," Mum shrieked, her head lolling, her words starting to slur. "But watched over by merteachers! Supervised! *Supervised!* AT ALL TIMES!"

"Very well, Kristabel," said Grandma. Then she turned – and pointed her wand straight at me.

Chapter 13

Submawitchery…

Now THAT is a magiskill I would *love* to have.

Not an ordinary magiskill. Not one like araknawitchery – one all witches can do, even if some witches do it better than others.

No.

One of the mega-magiskills. The *special* magiskills. The ones only some witches are born with. Only some witches can do…

Some lucky, LUCKY witches.

Because, as all you witchkids probably know, submawitchery is rare. *Very* rare. And I happen to know exactly how rare…

One witch – just ONE WITCH – in every *eight thousand, four hundred, and thirty-two witches* is born a submawitch.

My friend Kika is one of them. And so are most of Kika's family. Sometimes Kika's family spend whole *days* underwater, just swimming about, having fun.

I, sadly, am *not* a submawitch.

Which means being transformed into a creature who *can* breathe underwater – such as a woddelflomp – is the closest I get.

I flipped off down the sand, fast as I could – which was surprisingly speedy for something so small and stumpy. Then, like an arrow, I hurled myself into the water.

Straight away, I felt … well, at *home*. Breathing as easily as I do on land. Swimming about, using my strong flipper arms, waggling my strong flipper feet, zooming through the water much faster than I ever could as a witchkid.

But I also felt confused. And all you witchkids who have ever been transformed will know why. Because a tiny bit of my brain was still me – but a much MUCH bigger bit of my brain was woddelflomp.

And the me-bit of my brain knew I was there,

96

underwater, for a reason. But I just could NOT think what it was. Because the woddelflomp bit of my brain was thinking about something else...

About a long slimy strand of glistening green seaweed. And how very VERY tasty it looked.

With one snap – I munched it down.

The tiny me-bit of my brain was going *yuk yuk yuk, do NOT eat that*. But the woddelflomp-bit was snuffling with delight. Because it tasted chewy and salty and slimy and rubbery – and *delicious*.

In fact, it tasted so delicious I stuck a flipper out, grabbed another strand drifting past, and popped it in my pouch for later.

Then I started swimming further out, where the water got colder, and darker. Past the rocky island, past all sorts of fish swimming in and out of the coral.

And still I knew I was looking for something but I just could NOT remember what, so I kept on swimming.

I could hear noises all around me, under the sea. Noises you don't hear as a witchkid swimming under water.

Whistles and murmurs and booms and hisses and grunts and clicks and shrieks, and all sorts of chattering noises, one fish to another.

I swam past a sea unicorn – a boy, with lots of tiny eggs in his pouch. Swimming upright, bobbing gently along. Long bony tail curled up at the end, one twisted horn spiralling out of his head.

Then – darting up from behind a big rock on the seabed – a flash of grey. A camouflaged hunterfish. Big orange eyes on long stalks, two long sharp pincers.

It lunged, with deadly speed.

The sea unicorn had no chance. The hunterfish grabbed it and – with a swish of its tail – it was gone. Back behind the big rock again.

And the crunching noises began...

I gulped.

Then I spotted a flash of blue and yellow. Another woddelflomp.

Of course! *Now* I remembered why I was here.

Mervikk. That must be him. The only other woddelflomp around.

Then – whizzing through the water – came a small, bright-blue streak...

A *nibbet*.

Mervikk shot after it, flippers going as fast as they could. And I knew why.

Mervikk was mutant hunting. Hoping to find the SECOND mutant nibbet in Witchworld.

I shot after Mervikk. I could see, up ahead, the nibbet was panicking, checking over its shoulder, worrying about the woddelflomp on its tail. Worrying about being a woddelflomp dinner.

Then, ahead, far below, on the sea bed – a malakka shell. A big silvery shell. Wide open, with a little sea creature tucked inside.

The nibbet spotted it. It swerved, then headed straight down. Straight towards the malakka shell. Because the shell – it was refuge. A place to hide from a woddelflomp.

Because malakkas let nibbets take refuge in their shells. And in return, the nibbets pick grit off the malakkas.

Mervikk swerved to follow the nibbet. So close he could almost touch it. Then with one last swerve – the nibbet shot into the malakka shell. And the malakka shell snapped tight shut…

Right on Mervikk's front flipper.

Mervikk was STUCK. Stuck tight. And panicking. So was I.

I swam down, fast as I could. I pulled at Mervikk – HARD. I kicked at the shell. But I could NOT get it open.

Then, above us – the sea went dark. Dark with the long, long shadow of a huge black fish. A fish with billowing fins, like big black sails – and a long jagged saw for a snout.

A sawdredger. In search of its favourite food…

Woddelflomps.

The sawdredger spotted us. It turned. Its huge long body prepared to dive. Its jagged snout pointed down. Ready to SPEAR a woddelflomp on its long sharp end.

I pulled at Mervikk, harder and harder. I kicked at the shell. One last kick – so hard my flipper throbbed. Then – at last – the shell creaked open…

Just a *tiny* bit.

A tiny bit was enough.

Mervikk's flipper was out – and we were off. Swimming, as fast as we could. Heading back to the shallows, back to the beach. To *safety*.

Behind us the sawdredger swerved and cut its way through the water. It was gaining on us. Getting nearer and nearer and NEARER.

Then – we were in the shallows, swimming for the surface.

And Grandma was there. Sitting in a deck chair by her beach hut.

She spotted us straight away, flapping and floundering through the water to the beach.

She jumped up and ran – just as the sawdredger

pounced. Leapt out of the water behind us. Curved through the air and down, long sword-like snout stretched out to spear its dinner…

It missed Merivkk by CENTIMETRES.

Grandma hurled herself into the water and splashed towards the sawdredger. "SHOO!" she shrieked. "Shoo! SHOO! Go away!"

And the sawdredger turned and was gone.

Then me and Mervikk lay there, panting, on the beach. Wriggling and squirming, and feeling very strange. And then – transformed, just like me, from woddelflomp to witchkid – there he was.

Mervikk. Sitting on the beach – a bit dishevelled, a bit flushed. But beaming.

"Brilliant, Flo's-gran," he said, eyes shining. "Can I have another go?"

Chapter 14

Mum did a LOT of shrieking at Grandma once the jelly-legs spell wore off. She started shrieking down in the cove and she was still shrieking up in the garden.

Then she stopped.

Something was swooping towards Kronebay. Shooting through the sky. A huge skyrider. Long and sleek and pointed, like a silver shark in the sky.

"A *skysplitter*!" said Mervikk, jumping up and down. "Three times faster than any other skyrider! Only SIX skysplitters in the whole of Witchworld!"

And here it came.

Swooping across the whole of Kronebay in less than five seconds. Swooping straight towards the cliff top, straight towards us.

"It's going to crash," said Mum, panicking. "Right here! On the cliff!"

It didn't.

An earsplitting screech filled my ears and the skysplitter juddered to a halt. Stopped dead. In under one second.

Then it hovered, a vast shiny shape in the sky. And landed. Right in front of the only other house on the cliff top.

Jasmonikka Villa…

A huge house, pale yellow, set further back on the cliff. And covered in rambling jasmonikka – bright orange flowers just beginning to bloom.

We ran up the garden and stared.

The doors of the skysplitter swung open with a hiss, and down came a shiny silver staircase.

Then a long green carpet snaked out of the skysplitter and right up to the front door of Jasmonikka Villa.

And now – standing in the doorway of the skysplitter – was a witchman. He came strutting down the staircase. Then his voice boomed out.

"Settle me in, Stoop. Unpack my things," the

voice boomed. "But first – bring me a citrijuice to the west terrace. Three clumps of ice. One slice of zippel. And stir it three times. THREE times, Stoop. Not once, not twice – but *three* times. And bring me a bowl of Yumyums. But NOT the green ones. Take out *all* the green ones."

I stared. That strutting witchman, that booming voice – I knew who he was. Mr Potions2Go… Meristo Hurlstruk.

<hr />

"Meristo Hurlstruk!" Mum said, thrilled. "Here. Next door! This is a chance to *network*!"

"Network?" snorted Grandma. "Kristabel, what on earth do you mean by *network*?"

"I mean, Mother," said Mum, "that this is a business opportunity! And I shall use it. I shall develop the contact! Boost the profile of *Hocus Pocus*!"

"Develop the contact? Boost the profile?" snorted Grandma. "Really, Kristabel. Sometimes, even though I know perfectly well that you ARE speaking Witchen, I do *not* understand a single word you are saying. You might as well be speaking Lonaakkvrinkk."

Which, as you probably know, is a language no witches understand – except Lonelanders, of course.

Mum took no notice of Grandma. She was too

busy plotting and planning. "Meristo Hurlstruk is a powerful businesswitch," she said, eyes gleaming. "A useful contact. And all businesswitches must build contacts! Contacts in important places. Contacts who can pull strings. Get things done."

Now Mum was clasping her hands together. "Yes, yes, I see an opportunity to team up!" she said. "*Hocus Pocus* and Meristo Hurlstruk – doing good works. Just as *Scoop!* is doing!"

"Team up?" snorted Grandma. "I hardly think Meristo Hurlstruk will be keen to team up with you, Kristabel. Do you not remember your first meeting? What you DID?"

"I DO remember, Mother," said Mum.

So did I. I was there. In Mum's office. She was having a big important meeting – but Grandma interrupted it and made Mum cross. So cross she did araknawitchery on Grandma. Spun strong sticky thread out of her fingers, and cocooned Grandma in less than a minute.

Then she tucked Grandma – all cocooned, just her head sticking out – under one arm. She started screaming about how she was going to drop Grandma down a rubbish chute…

And THAT was when Mr Potions2Go walked in.

He was *not* impressed. He turned straight round and left.

"Mother," said Mum. "There has been a second meeting since that unfortunate incident. A power lunch for power witches. I explained the circumstances of your cocooning, and we had an exceedingly satisfactory conversation."

Mum's eyes glinted. "In fact," she said, "he understood very well – VERY WELL, Mother – that mothers can sometimes be *troublesome*."

Grandma snorted. But, to be fair, Mum's right. Grandma *can* be troublesome. Very troublesome.

And now Mum was walking fast across the front garden, towards Jasmonikka Villa, waving and peering over the fence.

"Meristo," she called. "Cooee! MERISTO! We meet again!"

As behind us – we heard a wail. A familiar wail.

Hetty.

She came stomping outside. "Calamity!" she wailed. "We had an ARRANGEMENT. Me, Errken. We were going to screenchat at five. But he's not there. NOT THERE!"

She threw herself down on the front step. "Where is he? *Where?*" she wailed. "Suppose something has happened to him?"

Then smoke started to come out of her ears. "An accident, he's had an accident – that's it, I'm sure!" she wailed. "There can be no other *possible* reason. Oh, where IS he?"

"Good riddance," said Grandma. "He's pompous and dull and a nitwit. You're better off without him."

Hetty's teeth started grinding. I could see she was about to shriek at Grandma – and I didn't blame her. Because that was really quite rude. Even if Grandma was right.

But then we heard the *putt putt putt* of a skyscooter. Hetty's head whipped up. And there, above us, was a witchboy – a witchteen – coming in for a landing, a big wide grin on his face.

✦

"Archie!" Hetty shrieked, hurling herself at him. "Archie!"

Archie. Archilon Blokk.

Archie lives in Kronebay all year round. He and Hetty met on the beach years ago. Both hunting for merhoppers in the rock pools. They've been friends ever since.

He hopped off his skyscooter – and Hetty's mouth dropped open. So did mine. So did Grandma's.

"Good gracious, Archie," said Grandma. "How very LANKY you have become. Has your mother been feeding you superspeedy growing potion?"

Because last time we were in Kronebay, Hetty and Archie were about the same height. But not now. Now Archie was a LOT taller than Hetty.

Hetty's eyebrows were knotting. "You've stretched, Archie," she said. "But not just that. You look … different. Older … but why? Is it the height? Or the hair?"

Last time Archie's hair was all scruffy and shaggy. But not this time. Now it was cut into a shape. A flopping sort of shape – and Hetty was nodding approvingly.

"It's the hair," she said. "Definitely the hair."

But now it was Archie who was staring. Peering at Hetty's face. "Hen," he said – which is what he always calls Hetty. "Turn … sideways."

Hetty looked at him. Gasped. "Archie," she said, twisting her head sideways, and grabbing on to his arm. "Can you see it? CAN you?"

Archie stared more. He started to nod. "I do believe I can," he said. "A hint. A tiny hint."

Hetty's face lit up. "Archie, I am SO happy!" she shrieked. "You *can* see it! You CAN!"

Now a grin started to stretch itself right across Archie's face – and Hetty spotted it.

"I know you think I worry way too much about

my nose," she shrieked. "But YOU try having a nose like mine — so small and neat and straight. But no more. NO MORE! Now, finally, it is going to be a *good* witchy nose. A *fine* witchy nose. The nose of my DREAMS!"

"Hen," said Archie. "Whatever happens to your nose — it makes NO difference to what I think of you…"

He paused. "Because I will ALWAYS think you are utterly ridiculous," he said.

Then he flicked Hetty's arm. "But never change, Hen," he said. "Never change."

He stopped. Took something out of his robe pocket and handed it to me. "Flo," he said, smiling down at me. "Thought you might like this. For your collection."

Chapter
15

It was a shell, a beautiful curved shell, that Archie gave me. All blues and greens and silvers – the shimmering colours of the Sheltered Sea.

I added it to my shell collection that night. All of them lined up on my bedroom window sill.

Mervikk was already fast asleep next door. With his door wide open, and the landing light on.

Because Mervikk told Mum that although sleeping in a very big room was excellent, it was not something he was used to – and he would very much prefer his door open and a light on.

I could see him lying, arms flung over his head.

Worn out and muttering. Busy dreaming about something – and I had a good idea what…

Mutants. Mutant nibbets.

Because Mervikk spent the last hour before bed hunting all round the house and garden for nibbets. Checking them ALL for signs of mutation…

I curled up in bed, smelling the fragrant vistarikka outside. Listening to the faint sounds of waves, washing backwards and forwards, up against the cliffs. And the chirruppellas calling to each other out in the garden.

Staring at the picture by my bed.

The framed picture. Of me and Dad on Witchen Day.

Me – dressed in my present from Mum, the complete Destiny Daggett outfit. The cape, the mask, the belt stuffed with *Skyhunter* kit.

Dad – smiling down at me. Holding out a parcel. A tiny parcel, wrapped in shiny gold paper.

And I lay there, remembering…

*

"Flo," said Dad, smiling down at me, as he held out a parcel. "This is my Witchen Day present to you."

And, as Mum clicked her skychatter and took the picture, I took the parcel. I stared down at it. Then unwrapped the shiny gold paper. Inside was a box.

A tiny gold box, with a tiny gold clasp.

I undid the clasp. Opened the box up.

And there – nestling in a bed of darkest green velvet – was a lantern. A tiny green lantern, not even as big as my hand. With a tiny green flame, a long green hook, and a dangling linked chain.

I stared down at it.

"It's beautiful," I said. And it was.

I picked it up, took it out of its soft velvet bed, and cupped it in my hand.

The lantern glowed. The flame flickered.

"It knows you. Knows you are a Valliant," Dad said, with a smile. "For this lantern, Flo, is a special thing. An heirloom."

"An heirloom?" I said.

"Passed down by Valliants, generation to generation," Dad said. "And now, Flo, this lantern – the lantern of the Valliants – it belongs to you."

"It looks very old, Daddy," I said.

"Flo, it is *ancient*," Dad said. "Passed from Valliant to Valliant for hundreds of years. The first known Valliant to own this lantern lived back in the days of Ancient Witchspeak."

I gasped. "That IS a long time ago," I said.

"Indeed it is," said Dad. "And all we know of that first Valliant comes from a painting. An ancient painting of a young witchgirl walking in a forest. Her face fearful, yet comforted by the light of the lantern she holds in her hand. *This* lantern, Flo. It is a most mysterious painting. With a title below it: *Kora Valliant walks in the forest, and waits*."

I stared at the lantern. "But the lantern," I said, "it's very small. How did it light the way for Kora Valliant?"

Dad smiled. "The lantern, the flame…" he said, "they are as big as a Valliant chooses."

Then he picked up the tiny lantern by its hook, and waved his hand.

I gasped. "Daddy, the lantern, it's *growing!*" I said.

"This lantern, Flo," Dad said. "Can be small as your hand, or tall as a tree. For it is a MAGIC lantern."

He handed the lantern to me – and I stared. At the lantern, much bigger now, swinging from my hands.

"The flame, too," Dad said, "will do as a Valliant wishes."

Then he waved his hand and the flame grew brighter. Brighter and brighter. Sending light – dazzling light – soaring across the room.

"That picture, Daddy," I said, pointing. "What's that?"

There, above the flame of the lantern, was a

picture. An engraving, carved into the metal. A flame, cupped in two curved hands. With writing around it.

"That, Flo," said Dad, "is the special sign of the Valliants."

"And the writing," I said, "what does it mean?"

Because I could read the words – but they made no sense…

Sempora Lumarin
Sempora Sperokkin

"Sempora Lumarin, Sempora Sperokkin," said Dad. "Words in Ancient Witchspeak. The motto of the Valliants. 'Forever Light, Forever Hope'."

Then he smiled. "For while there is one flicker of light in the lantern of the Valliants –" he said, "then so must there be one flicker of hope in the heart of a Valliant."

✦

I lay there, remembering that Witchen Day. Remembering the lantern of the Valliants. Remembering everything Dad told me about it.

How the flame was not real – but a magical flame. The look of fire – yet not real fire. How the flame burned, day and night, just as it had for hundreds of years. How it never, EVER went out.

Remembering Dad showing me how to control the size of the lantern, the strength of the flame. All with my hands.

Remembering Dad showing me how I could hook the tiny lantern to a belt or a button. So the lantern could travel with me, anywhere I chose.

Remembering Dad telling me the code – the secret code of the Valliants. How each letter had its own secret code. A code of short and long flares of the flame, with spaces between. How to count the flares and the spaces – shorter spaces between letters, longer spaces between words.

How, as a young witchboy, he would be roaming the hills, then see beams of light flashing through the darkening sky. The lantern of the Valliants spelling out a message from his mother, again and again…

COME HOME
COME HOME

And now – the lantern was here. Hanging by its hook here in my room in Kronebay.

I stared at the lantern, at the gentle, flickering flame. And slowly, slowly, my eyes began to close.

And that night, in my dreams, I dreamt of Dad. Of his voice.

"I will be back, Flo," I dreamt his voice was saying, again and again. "I WILL be back. And *soon*."

Chapter 16

"Mother," said Mum next morning. "I am off for a Seaweed Soak at Kronebay Spa. Followed by a Watery Workout."

Then Hetty came in. Wearing another two-piece – black and sporty, with running shoes on her feet. "I have decided," she said, "this week is an *opportunity*. For me to develop a Glow. A Glow through exercise and beauty treatments. And when I go back, Errken will be dazzled by my Glow. Then – FINALLY – Errken will be my boyfriend."

"He's an idiot," said Grandma. "You're well matched."

"Mother," said Mum, while Hetty glared at Grandma. "Hetty and I shall be gone some hours. Kindly observe these three rules."

She pointed her spellstick. "*Abrakkida Rune*," she said, and a sheet of paper flew into the kitchen and stuck itself to the wall. With Mum's big scrawly writing on it:

NO DANGEROUS ACTIVITIES
NO ILLEGAL ACTIVITIES
NO GETTING ARRESTED

"Kristabel," said Grandma, offended. "Have you no eyes? Can you not see? I am baking. BAKING."

Which she was, with Mervikk as her helper. Mervikk was already hard at work. Wearing a chef's hat, sifting flour into a big bowl.

Because it turned out that Mervikk was an expert baker. "Dad loves cakes," Mervikk told Grandma. "I make them all the time."

"Mervikk," said Grandma, holding out a teaspoon of filling. "Taste this. What do you think?"

Mervikk took the spoon. "A touch more citrizest, Flo's-gran," he said.

An hour later, the cake was ready, and smelling VERY tasty.

Grandma packed it in a big basket. "We shall picnic at the Falls," she said – just as something big and yellow and hairy flashed across the garden. Something with wild hair and three heads. Something riding a broomstick the size of a tree...

I knew what it was straight away.

The Trigoggladron.

"Wahey, Flo's-gran! THIS is the way to travel!" Mervikk whooped, squashed between Grandma and me on Grandma's biggest broomstick.

He took to broomstick riding the moment he jumped on. He wasn't a bit scared or nervous. Not like I was the first time...

Like I was *now*.

I clung on behind Mervikk, as Grandma swooped and swerved after the Trigoggladron. Dashing through fields, woodlands – chasing after the flashes of yellow ahead of us.

But then – disaster...

A huge flutter of fairies came swooping towards us through the sky, looking terrified. They swooped by, tiny wings fluttering as fast as they could.

Then, behind them, we saw it – a blur whizzing past. A *huge* blur. Chasing after them.

I had no idea what it was. It was going so fast.

A huge blur of colours. All sorts of colours. Red and blue and green and yellow. With big flappy wings and huge orange antlers waggling on its head. Making the strangest shrieking, squawking noises – deafening noises – and passing so close its wing feathers brushed against my robes.

And – whatever it was – the broomstick did NOT like it.

It started spinning round and round. Shooting forwards, shooting backwards. Jumping sideways. Jerking and jolting and panicking.

"SPOOKED! The poor little thing is spooked!" shouted Grandma, tussling with the broomstick. "Hold on tight. Everything is under control!"

It did NOT feel like everything was under control. The broomstick was bucking and jumping. Then it spun round and headed back the way we'd come…

Straight into the path of a skyscudder coming from the opposite direction.

"Grandma!" I shouted. "Watch out!"

I could hear a voice, an angry voice, yelling at us to get out of the way. So could Grandma. She did an emergency swerve – but so did the skyscudder.

There was a crunch, and a huge jolt. I felt myself hurled off the broomstick and flying through the air. Then – with a thud – I crash-landed on the ground.

Along with Grandma, Mervikk, the broomstick…
And the skyscudder.

✳

An old witchman staggered out of the skyscudder –
a shock of grey hair sticking right up on end. Bushy
grey eyebrows knotted over glaring grey eyes.

"Nincompoop!" he roared, right in Grandma's
face. "Watch where you're GOING! Broomsticks
give way to skyriders. First rule of the skyways!"

"It is you – YOU! – who is the nincompoop!"
Grandma roared back. "How could I give way? You
were coming straight at me!"

They squared up to each other. He was bright
green now, and spitting with rage. So was Grandma.

"You shouldn't be in charge of one of those
skyrider thingies at all!" bellowed Grandma.
"A witchman your age – you should stick to a
broomstick!"

"You, you…! A boiled striggle egg would ride a
broomstick better than you!" he bellowed back.

And just when I thought he and Grandma were
going to kill each other – they stopped. Peered at
each other. Gaped. Then they spoke.

"Gilbert Grittokk?" said Grandma.

"Dorabel Skritchett?" said the witchman.

For a moment – one moment only – I thought

the argument was over. But it wasn't.

Grandma stared, then stared more. And so did the witchman. Then they both started glaring again. And bellowing.

"You were a sneaky little witchgirl, Dorabel Skritchett," the witchman bellowed. "And you are NO DIFFERENT now."

"Hah!" bellowed Grandma. "You, Gilbert Grittokk – you were an odious little witchboy, and I see that NOTHING HAS CHANGED!"

Then Grandma pointed her wand and shouted magic words. And a shower of stardust shot out of her wand, and swirled around the witchman.

"Take that, Gilbert Grittokk!" Grandma shrieked, as his hair turned purple, then green, then blue, then orange. "Take that!"

"Grandma, STOP!" I said. "That's illegal witch-harming magic!"

"Who cares?" Grandma shouted. "Not me!"

"Nor me!" Gilbert bellowed back, pulling out his wand and shouting magic words. "Nor me!"

And, just as a pair of chunky silver antlers appeared out of nowhere and stuck themselves to Grandma's head, I heard the sound of sirens.

Witchwarden sirens…

Chapter 17

Grandma gave the witchman one last glare. Then she grabbed me and Mervikk and ran for the broomstick – and the witchman ran for his skyscudder.

"Grandma," I shouted over Mervikk's shoulder, as the broomstick zoomed away from the ground. "Who was that witchman? Why are you so CROSS with him?"

Grandma ignored me. "Hold on tight!" she shouted, antlers waggling. "Next stop – the Falls!"

The Rainbow Falls… My favourite picnic spot. A beautiful spot.

A sloping meadow inland from Kronebay. The

River Dash running down from the hills above. Splashing over rocks, tumbling down and down – the light of the suns catching the splashes, and turning them all the colours of the rainbow as they fall.

"Grandma," I said, as we landed. "How long will you have silver antlers for?"

"Depends on that silly witchman and his spell," said Grandma huffily, hopping off the broomstick. But just then – PING! The antlers were gone.

"But who *was* he?" I said.

Grandma stuck her nose in the air. "I shall fill up our water bottles," she said, "with the fresh clear water of the Falls." And she marched off towards the river.

It was *very* puzzling. They knew each other, Grandma and that witchman – that was clear. But it was also clear that, for some reason, Grandma was NOT going to talk about it.

Mervikk, on the other hand, couldn't *stop* talking – about the creature that spooked the broomstick.

"A mutant," he said, eyes shining. "It was DEFINITELY a mutant. My first mutant!"

I gaped.

"That bird, that *creature* – its eyes were glowing," he said. "Glowing bright green. Green beams coming right out of them. ZZZUUUUM! In two straight lines. Like lasers. And there is not one creature in the whole of Witchworld that has glowing green eyes…"

He paused, eyes shining. "Not one creature…" he said, "*except* for that MUTANT NIBBET!"

"Mervikk," I said. "That thing, that creature – it did NOT have glowing green eyes."

I didn't actually *see* its eyes, not from where I was – just the flappy wings and orange antlers – but it was obviously nonsense.

"I could see it better than you could," Mervikk insisted. "And I tell you – it had glowing green eyes. And it flew off out to sea, towards the Wild Isles. So maybe it's on Kraggen. Maybe we can track it down!"

Just then Grandma came back from the Falls. "*Abrakkida Terratik, Mensalikkon Rubik,*" she said, waving her wand. "*Ederrik, Kibillika, Stune.*"

A shower of stardust swirled round the picnic basket. The lid opened up. A checked tablecloth flew out and spread itself on the ground. Then plates, knives, forks, food – they all followed. And arranged themselves on the tablecloth.

And, best of all, Mervikk was too busy eating to talk about mutants.

Until, that is, he ate some pippel fruit…

There's a big clump of pippel trees on the edge of the meadow. All groaning with pippel fruits. And Grandma always picks some when we go to the Falls.

She did today.

She stood under a pippel tree, pointed both arms straight above her head, then zoomed up in the air. She hovered right near the top of the tree – because that's where pippel fruits grow – and picked a big bunch.

Then she zoomed back down.

Mervikk was impressed. "Flo's-gran," he said. "That was excellent leviwitchery."

"Thank you, Mervikk," said Grandma. "I was quite the champion in my day. Finest leviwitch in class. Still got the magiskills."

You've probably felt the first stirrings of leviwitchery yourself. Most witchkids our age have. Maybe you've felt a bit bouncy, or a bit itchy under the feet… Maybe you've even done the occasional tiny take-off from the ground…

Well, here in United Witchenlands we are NOT encouraged to develop our leviwitchery. Not until we're a certain weight and height. Usually around age fourteen.

And even then, we can only try out leviwitchery with a qualified teacher and the proper safety equipment. That's the rules.

But Mervikk had other ideas. "Flo's-gran," he said. "Can you teach me leviwitchery?"

"Mervikk," I said. "NO. We're not old enough. Not tall enough. And not heavy enough. It's not safe."

Grandma snorted. "Witch Wellbeing and Safety," she said. "Bunch of mimsies. At your age I was already picking pippel fruits."

"But Grandma," I said, "there were a lot of witchkids in your day who did leviwitchery and FLOATED AWAY. Were never seen again."

"No risk, no gain," said Grandma firmly. "But sadly, Mervikk, at your age – you will most probably need booster potion to do leviwitchery. And I have none with me."

Then Grandma got out a pippelpeeler – one of the tiniest domestic imms. And the pippelpeeler zoomed round all the pippel fruits, peeling the skin off.

Mervikk was staring. "I've never had pippel fruit," he said. "Never even *seen* it."

"Mervikk, you are in for a treat," said Grandma.

"It is a delicacy. Delicious. Once tasted, never forgotten. So tuck in."

So Mervikk *did* tuck in. But straight away, something happened. Spots — bright orange, the exact colour of a pippel — popped up all over his face. Then his arms, then his legs. His hair shot up on end, and his ears started to grow leaves. Pippel tree leaves.

"Wh-wh-what's happening?" Mervikk said, eyes popping. "What's happening to me?"

"Keep calm, Mervikk," said Grandma. "You are merely REACTING. Allergic." And she whipped a small potion bottle out of her handbag. "Three drops of this should sort you out."

And it did. The spots faded, the hair flopped, the leaves withered, then dropped off Mervikk's ears.

"Interesting, Mervikk," Grandma said. "Very few witches have an allergic reaction to pippel fruit. It seems you are one of them."

Which set Mervikk off about mutants *again*... Because when me and Mervikk went and dabbled our feet in the Falls while Grandma had a short snooze — Mervikk had ANOTHER idea about mutants.

"That's it!" said Mervikk. "That's how mutants happen. It's the Allergics!"

Mervikk was nodding now. "Like me and the pippel fruit. I reacted. You didn't. That's how mutants work, most probably. Some creatures react to the magic, some don't. So that mutant I saw, it must have been an Allergic, and—"

I *had* to stop him. So I butted in.

"Mervikk," I said. "You don't *know* you saw a mutant. You *think* you did. Maybe it was a new species."

Because new species are discovered quite often in Witchworld. Last week they discovered a new kind of squid in the Deepwaters, not far from Loneland.

Now Mervikk was shaking his head from side to side – vigorously, like a windsniffer shaking itself dry after a wallow. "No species has glowing green eyes," said Mervikk, and he got this stubborn look on his face.

Then he grabbed my arm. "And you know what else, Flo?" he said. "Leviwitchery – that'd be a useful skill for a mutant hunter. You could dodge a mutant. Get out of the way of a mutant. Say a mutant was coming towards you - *Whoosh!* You could—"

"Mervikk, shush," I said, and I put my hand over his mouth. "Can we talk about something else? Something that *isn't* mutants? It's getting BORING."

But I wasn't just bored. There was more.

Because each time Mervikk talked about mutants, a picture popped into my head – that small hissing nibbet with the glowing green eyes. And each time, it made me shiver…

Mervikk did try.

The rest of the day he tried. Each time he started to talk about mutants – he stopped himself. But I could see he was still thinking about them.

So I suppose I shouldn't have been surprised by what happened next morning…

Chapter 18

Next morning, voices woke me – down in the garden. I looked out of my window, and there was Mervikk. Halfway down the garden, and strapped into a harness, attached by a rope to the bottom of our latchenboll tree.

Grandma was out there too, giving Mervikk a spoonful of potion.

Potion…

Oh no. Oh no no NO.

I had a horrible idea I knew what kind of potion it was.

Booster potion.

Now Grandma was scampering back towards the terrace. Towards the latchenboll tree. Then she started shouting instructions. "Time for take-off, Mervikk!" she shouted. "Assume the position!"

Take-off...

The latchenboll tree was blowing about in the wind. It looked like a very gusty day and I had a VERY bad feeling about this.

The window – I *had* to get it open. Had to STOP them.

But the window was jammed. A bit open at the bottom but, however hard I pushed, I just could NOT open it more.

Now Grandma was standing by the latchenboll tree, feet together, arms above her head, fingers pointing straight upwards.

Down the garden, Mervikk did the same.

And *still* the window wouldn't open. It was jammed tight – which it does sometimes, especially after rain. But why now? NOW?

"Close your eyes, Mervikk!" shouted Grandma. "Think LIGHT! Think STRAIGHT! Think STRONG! Think happy thoughts – of pelloligans soaring, of zizzwings swooping. Think like a bird! Think like a rocket! Feel lightness! Feel strength! Feel it through your feet. Feel it through your whole body!"

Now something was happening to Mervikk. He was starting to bounce, then bounce more.

"Lighter, Mervikk!" shouted Grandma. "Think LIGHTER! Think STRONGER! And have no fear – the harness will stop you if you go too high."

Now Mervikk was shooting up in to the air, eyes popping, arms flailing, legs scrabbling. "I'm doing it, Flo's-gran!" he whooped. "I'm doing it!"

At last! The window opened. I had to STOP this.

"Grandma!" I shouted. "GRANDMA!"

"Not now, Flo," she said, waving an arm at me. "Mervikk is under instruction!"

"But Grandma – the rope!" I shouted. Because I could see what Grandma couldn't. A chirruppella, right by the latchenboll tree. With its teeth round the rope. Gnawing with its sharp little teeth.

And with all that chewing, the rope – the only thing attaching Mervikk to the ground – was looking very VERY frayed…

Then – SNAP! The rope broke.

The startled chirruppella ran – straight at Grandma, shot through her legs, and tripped her up. While Mervikk carried on hurtling upwards.

Up and up Mervikk went. Kicking his legs, flapping his arms, trying desperately to stop himself.

It was no good. He could NOT stop.

"Help!" he shrieked. "Stop me! Help!"

I froze. Panicked. What to do?

Grandma was struggling to her feet, searching for her wand. Mervikk was going higher and higher – a tiny speck now, way up in the sky. He couldn't stop. Any second now, he'd be out of sight.

Or – just as bad – what if he DID stop? Then started hurtling *downwards*? Then what?

Mum. I'd get Mum. She could chase him, stop him. Or catch him on the way down. Do something. *Anything*.

Then I remembered – Mum was with her personal witchtrainer. Running on the beach in Kronebay.

But then – out of nowhere – a skyscudder came zooming towards Mervikk. The flexipod opened – and a long bony arm reached out, grabbed Mervikk, and pulled him inside.

Then the skyscudder turned. Pointing downward, heading for our garden.

I slumped. Mervikk was safe.

The skyscudder landed, right beside Grandma. And Mervikk hopped out, grinning. Then a furious face looked out of the flexipod.

The witchman. Gilbert Grittokk.

"Dorabel Skritchett," he bellowed. "I might have

known you were behind this! You are even more of a NINCOMPOOP now than you were as a witchchild!"

And the skyscudder took off and was gone.

✳

Mervikk and Grandma walked up the garden and into the house.

I ran down to meet them. Mervikk was running round and round the sitting room in small circles. Babbling. Shocked. Thrilled.

"Flo's-gran," he said. "I did it, I did it! I went WHEEEEE! Up and up and—"

Then he collapsed. "My legs," he said. "They're not working. Look."

Now Mervikk's knees were knocking. His teeth started clacking. His face went pale green. "I feel sick," he said.

Then he started waving his arms, eyes huge and staring. "I feel like I'm … *robes* … spinning round and round in a witchwasher. Round and round and round and round and—"

"Hmm," said Grandma. "Mervikk, I rather fear you have some form of Shocks."

Then she pointed her wand, said lots of magic words, and stardust swirled all around Mervikk.

His eyes went wide. He stopped talking, stopped

moving, he looked as if he was in some sort of trance. Then he lifted off the ground and floated towards the sitting-room door.

"He'll be tucked up in bed in a jiffy," said Grandma. "A snooze will soon set him right."

I glared at Grandma. "Grandma," I said – and I couldn't help it, I found myself wagging my finger at her. "You were lucky he was rescued. He is in our care. You REALLY should have more sense of responsibility. *Anything* could have happened!"

"Oh, pish," said Grandma – but she had a guilty look in her eye, and she was scuffing her foot on the floor.

"It is ONLY because of that witchman that Mervikk is still here," I said.

Grandma hung her head, scuffed her foot more. "Just a shame his rescuer had to be Gilbert Grittokk," she muttered. Which I thought was VERY ungrateful of her.

"Grandma," I said. "Gilbert Grittokk just saved Mervikk. Who *is* he? How do you know him? And what COULD he have done to make you so cross?"

"Flo," said Grandma, sticking her nose in the air. "Since you simply will not stop asking questions about that irritating witchman – I shall SHOW you."

Chapter 19

I stared. "Grandma," I said. "Is that a *memory ball*?"

"It is," said Grandma proudly. "I never travel without it."

Grandma patted it. "Built to last," she said. "Olden-day witches – they knew how to build magical things. They used care. Craftsmanship."

Grandma waved her hands over it. It started to shimmer and glow. A soft golden glow.

I stared more. I've seen memory balls in the Haggspit Museum of Witchhistory. Room 54. But only behind glass, and never working.

Witches don't need them now – not now

memories are streamed straight to the witchfixer.

But this – this was beautiful.

"At my age, a witch has so many memories. And all gathered here," said Grandma. "I never tire of looking through."

I watched, amazed, as golden stardust swirled out of the ball, and around Grandma's head.

"Flo," said Grandma, as the stardust shimmered and glowed. "I shall show you my first meeting with Gilbert Grittokk."

I looked into the shimmering ball. At a long line of tiny witches, flying two-by-two on broomsticks – a suitcase strapped to the back of each broomstick.

"There," said Grandma, pointing at a small witchgirl, ringlets bobbing under her hat. "That's me. And that little witchboy flying next to me, that's Gilbert. Both evacuees."

Mr Prankett told us about evacuees in witchhistory. How witchkids – lots of them – were sent out of the cities in the Second Wand War. Sent to the country, where it was safer. Separated from their witchmums and dads. Not knowing how long they'd be gone, or who they'd be living with.

"See that," said Grandma, pointing to a mask slung round her neck. "My magic mask – in case of poison powder attack!"

Grandma waved her hands, and the memory ball shimmered. Now she and Gilbert, and all the other tiny witchkids, were lining up in a shabby building.

"Those grown-ups," she said, pointing, "they were choosing which of us to take in."

I stared. Some of those grown-up witches looked kind and friendly – but not all.

"See that one," Grandma said, pointing at a very grumpy, mean-looking witch. "We did NOT want her to choose us."

Then Grandma cackled. "So we made sure she didn't."

I looked. The tiny Grandma was scratching her head very hard. "I pretended I had nits," Grandma cackled. And beside her, I could see the tiny Gilbert sticking his finger up his nose, and wiggling it about.

Grandma waved her hand again. "We were chosen by farmer witches," she said. Then she sighed. "Such happy days."

Images shimmered past. Grandma and Gilbert playing in a big field of something. Helping with the skrumpel harvest. Chasing each other through a field of tall grass.

"Us city witchchildren knew nothing of the country," Grandma said. "But we soon learned. And we loved it. The fresh air, the nature. Gilbert especially. By the end of that year he could name every plant, every tree."

"But Grandma," I said. "You and Gilbert... You seem good friends there."

"We were," said Grandma. "Until the day before we left. We found the skull of a bobbentuft. I wanted to take it home as a souvenir. Gilbert too. We had a row. A tussle. The skull broke. Then – we had a spell fight."

It was quite a spell fight.

Two little witchkids making each other shrink. Giving each other long tails and extra noses...

I can see why we have laws now, about witchkids and magic – even if Grandma ignores most of them.

"We never made up," Grandma said. "I said Gilbert should say sorry first. But Gilbert – that obstinate stubborn witchboy – he said I should. Me! ME!"

Grandma's eyes were popping indignantly. "We never spoke again," she said. "And we left the next day. Never kept in touch."

I gaped. What a STUPID reason to stop being friends. And they were still cross about it? They were as stubborn, as idiotic as each other.

But I didn't say that. I didn't want to annoy Grandma because I had something VERY important to ask her.

"Grandma," I said. "Will you show me Dad in your memory ball?"

✳

Grandma did. She showed me the very first meeting between her and Dad. Mum, looking nervous. But Dad not looking nervous at all. Going straight up to Grandma. Shaking her hand, and asking her something.

I stared and stared.

Mum, Dad – both looking so young. So happy.

"He asked me about my wand," Grandma said. "Wanted to know all about it. Asked so many things."

I stared more. Sometimes I watch our old family witchfliks. Ones of all of us. But this – this was Mum and Dad before I was born. Before Hetty was born.

Grandma waved her hand again. "This, Flo, you should see," she said.

I stared. Mum and Dad's wedding. The two of them, standing in a meadow. Next to a woldenbore tree. All their friends and family. Faces I recognised, but younger. And faces of witches I had never met. All smiling. Showering Mum and Dad with fluttering petals of coloured paper that turned into shimmerwings and flew away.

"See how happy they look?" said Grandma.

Now Mum and Dad were running through a line of witches, broomsticks raised to create an archway.

Then – we heard a gasp from the doorway behind us.

Mum.

She was standing there. Staring at the memory ball. "Oh," she said, both cheeks flushing bright green.

"See that, Kristabel," said Grandma. "Remember that day? All those high hopes? How, just afterwards – you told me it was the wisest thing you had ever done in your life? Well it WAS. And when Lyle returns you must—"

"Mother," Mum said, and rings of smoke started puffing out of her ears. "Stop. STOP!"

But Grandma didn't. She wagged a finger right in Mum's face. "Kristabel," she said, "you had better start thinking about what you are going to say to him on his return."

Grandma snorted. "That divorce," she said. "Biggest mistake you two nincompoops ever made."

Mum sat herself down at a breakfast-bar stool, glaring. "You made us do it," she said, and I could hear her teeth grinding. "You and Hetty."

"We had to," said Grandma. "The pair of you

142

were IMPOSSIBLE to live with back then. All that shouting. All those silly spells."

Hetty told me about Mum and Dad's big rows. Yelling at each other, and doing illegal witch-harming spells on each other. Giving each other big purple rashes. Or long swishing tails. One time Mum turned Dad in a five-eared grifflehonk, so he turned her into a three-nosed hoggelsnort.

So, when I was three, Hetty stole Mum and Dad's spellsticks. Then Grandma stuck Mum and Dad in a cage full of two-headed grinthogs. Said they could only come out if they promised to divorce.

"You had NO sense whatsoever back then," Grandma said, tutting. "You failed to see what you had. But now – you are FAR less silly. You are growing up at last. Now you are ready."

Smoke rings were coming out of Mum's ears now. Small, but growing bigger. "Mother," she said, grinding her teeth. "I suggest you stop talking. RIGHT THIS MINUTE."

"I shall NOT," said Grandma, eyes popping. "Lyle Skritchett was the only witchman who was ever honest. Who saw you for who you were. And despite all your silly, foolish ways – he STILL loved you."

Mum started hissing. Now smoke was pouring out of her ears. Force 5 fumawitchery – at *least*.

But just then Mervikk came in to the room.

"I'm better now, Flo's-gran," he said, beaming. "TOTALLY over the Shocks. And over the harness snapping. So when can I have my next leviwitchery lesson?"

Mum's teeth began to grind. "Next leviwitchery lesson?" she hissed, right in Grandma's face. "Next *LEVIWITCHERY LESSON*?"

Chapter 20

Mum and Grandma had one of their big rows – the kind Hetty calls the Humdingers. Lots of screeching from Mum, lots of bellowing from Grandma, and LOTS of fumawitchery.

They stopped in the end. Then Grandma marched off to her room, while Mum flopped down into an armchair.

"Mervikk," she said, "I am so sorry you had to hear that unfortunate … *discussion*."

"Oh, I enjoyed hearing it, Flo's-mum," beamed Mervikk. "And I'm speaking to Dad tomorrow – at LAST – and I can't *wait* to tell him about the leviwitchery, and the harness snapping. And about being a woddelflomp, and the sawdredger!"

Mum went palest green. She bit her lip, and her eyes swivelled sideways. "Mervikk," she said. "I think it would be best if you did NOT mention those things. I rather think … if you do … you might be taken away from us. And my mother… She might be … er … *arrested*. So … not a word. Not to your father."

"Not tell Dad?" Mervikk said, eyes popping. "But – Flo's-mum, that's too hard. I have NEVER done so much fun stuff in my whole life as I've done since we got to Kronebay."

"And you shall do *more* fun stuff, Mervikk," said Mum, sounding a bit weary. "In fact – you shall pick the fun stuff to do today. A treat. A *safe* treat. One on which I shall accompany you. One you CAN tell your father about."

The moment Mum said that I knew what Mervikk would choose – and he did.

A trip out to the Wild Isles…

In search of *mutants*.

"Kristabel," Grandma said, nose in the air. "I shall not be joining you on the trip."

"No," hissed Mum, also sticking her nose in the

air. "You will not be joining us. Because you are not *invited*."

Grandma glared. "You try to educate a witchchild, do a good deed – and what happens? You get shouted at," she said sulkily.

"While we are out," hissed Mum, "you can do another good deed. You can set the pooperscooper to work. Get it to clean all the chirruppella poop-pats off the terrace."

Then I heard wailing – and Hetty came in. "Nooo!" she wailed. "Errken has DUMPED me – even BEFORE he was my boyfriend!"

She threw herself into a chair, grinding her teeth. "He is going on a date with Veracity! VERACITY!"

She sniffed. "But why not me? WHY? I did everything right. I spent *hours* listening to stupid Amadeo Mizzotti and his STUPID music. I learnt the names of every premier league gripball team. I pretended to like ALL the things Errken liked. And did Veracity bother? Did she go to all that *effort*? No! She even told Errken she didn't LIKE Amadeo Mizzotti! *Or* gripball! So how could he choose her? *How?*"

"Hm," said Grandma. "Perhaps he's not quite the idiot I thought."

Luckily, Hetty was wailing, so she didn't hear.

"My heart is broken," she wailed.

Then she slumped, head in hand. "I am DOOMED" she hissed, "never to have a boyfriend."

Just then there was a knock, and Archie's head popped round the door. "Anyone home?" he said.

Hetty rushed and grabbed him. "Archie, we are going to Kraggen and YOU are coming with us," she said.

"I am?" he said, looking baffled – then pleased.

"Yes," said Hetty. "Because Errken has – *foolishly* and *mistakenly*, Archie – decided NOT to be my boyfriend. And *you* are going to help me change his mind."

"I am?" said Archie again, looking more baffled – but less pleased.

"Yes," said Hetty. "I'll take Kwikpiks. LOTS of Kwikpiks. You, me, having a good time. Then Errken will see them. Feel *jealous*! Realise that I am a fun and interesting witchteen. That I am a CATCH."

A look flickered in Archie's eyes. I had no idea what the look was, but it was gone in a second. "Hen," he said. "If Errken has any sense – any sense *at all* – he will already know that."

The Wild Isles… Four hundred small islands,

stretching up through the Sheltered Sea and into the Northern Wildwaters. Small islands, but with lots of rare plants on them, ones that don't grow anywhere else in Witchworld.

The Wild Isles are a Protected Place now. But they weren't always.

Back in the olden days, witches went trampling all over the Wild Isles, digging up lots of the plants. Then witchboffins made an exciting discovery. One Wild Isle plant – pungent clumpweed – seemed to solve the problem of tooth rot in witches.

But then – *disaster*. The witchboffins went back to the Wild Isles. Back to the island where they found the pungent clumpweed ... and it was gone. Every single plant was GONE. Withered and died. Destroyed by a creeping fungus. Fungus brought to the island on the shoes of witches.

And *that* was when things changed. When witches realised it was vital to look after the Wild Isles. To protect and preserve them. To keep them safe. Untouched. Unspoilt. With a chance to recover, and to flourish.

So the Unity of Colonies declared the Wild Isles a Protected Place. Protected by the Shimmering – a magicreation, a protective magic shield around all the Wild Isles. Twenty-four hours a day, every day.

No seariders or skyriders can get through the Shimmering – only creatures.

There is *one* Wild Isle outside the Shimmering, though. Just one that witchtourists are allowed to visit…

Kraggen.

Mervikk told Mum all about his plans for Kraggen. "Me and Flo, we're going mutant hunting," he beamed, as the searider zoomed away from Kronebay and out towards Kraggen.

Then he unfurled the drawing he'd done of the weird creature. "We're hunting this," he said. "It's something we saw – and I am SURE it's a mutant, like that nibbet in the Wild Witchglobe report."

Now – I have no idea what I expected Mum to say. But not this.

Because Mum took a close look at the drawing. "Hm," she said thoughtfully. "A most interesting creature. Those claws… Your creature is probably a tree climber, Mervikk – using those claws to clamber up the trunk. And that beak… Your creature is probably an insect hunter. Using its beak like a chisel. To tap at the trees and find insects inside."

And when we got to Kraggen, Mum led the way.

"Your creature will go for the trees with the softest wood," she told Mervikk. "Perhaps the weeper trees. So we should head for the river."

We started walking. Then we heard a chattering noise in the trees. Tiny little birds with four spotted wings.

Straight away, Mum looked up. "Lesser-spotted chukkels," she said. "Warning other chukkels of danger. Of a predator in the area."

"A predator?" Mervikk said eagerly. "Could the predator be my creature?"

Mum shook her head. "Not this time, Mervikk," she said. "Chukkels use different calls to warn of different predators and this…" She stopped, listened hard.

"This," she said, "is warning of a moss serpent."

And sure enough – a small green serpent came slithering out of the undergrowth.

Mum was like that all morning. Full of knowledge about creatures and plants as she helped Mervikk with his mutant hunting.

And that was a BIG surprise to me, so when we stopped by the lagoon for a picnic I asked her. "Mum…" I said. "All this stuff – how do you know it?"

"Flo, I used to come here with your father," she

said. "When we were courting. We used to hike all over Kraggen. He taught me many things about our wild world."

Then she looked thoughtful. "I had forgotten how much I enjoy a hike," she said. "A simple hike."

So that was the first surprise on Kraggen – Mum. But it wasn't the ONLY surprise that day. There was a second surprise in store – a BIG surprise – straight after the picnic…

Chapter 21

"*Abrakkida Rune*," Mum said, pointing her spellstick at the picnic hamper. The lid opened and out flew a tablecloth. Then bowls of food, and cartons of drink, and knives and forks, and plates and cups.

Then, just as the last plates flew on to the tablecloth – we heard the stomp of stout boots. Hetty and Archie, back from the Two-Hour Trail around Kraggen.

"Hiking is excellent exercise," said Hetty happily, "and most *definitely* a way to increase my Glow. And all the fresh air – that must be helping my Glow."

Then she flopped down on the picnic rug,

and Archie flopped beside her. "And hiking is surprisingly enjoyable," Hetty said thoughtfully. "Even with *no point* to the hiking. No SHOPS at the end of it. Just hiking in a big circle – nothing to do but spot flowers, and chat."

She patted Archie on the knee. "And it's very RELAXING being with you, Archie," she said. "Not having to *pretend* I like the things you like. Not worrying that the sea air is making my hair go frizzy."

"Thank you, Hen," said Archie.

Then he shuffled a bit on the rug. "*Premonition 2* is on at the witchfliks this week," he said, staring *very* hard at a blade of grass on the rug. "I thought maybe you … me … we could go and see it?"

"Oh yes!" said Hetty. "Brilliant!"

"Brilliant?" said Archie, looking pleased.

"Absolutely," said Hetty. "Then I can take a Kwikpik outside Kronebay Skyscreen. Or two! Or *three*! Then Errken will be SEETHING with jealousy. And Errken will realise his TRUE feelings – which are for *me*, not Veracity. And finally – FINALLY – he will ask me out on a date when I get back."

I heard a sound then – which I think came from Archie. A small exasperated sort of sigh.

154

After the picnic, Hetty and Archie went to do the Cliff Top Clamber. Mum magicreated herself a comfy chair, and settled down to read.

And me and Mervikk went for a paddle in the lagoon. And THAT was when the second surprise happened. Right there, by the lagoon.

✳

"You never know," Mervikk said, sounding hopeful. "That mutant could be a *wader* of some kind. We might find clawprints in the sand. Leading to its nest. And it might build its nest in rocks, like cloudswoopers do. THIS could be the moment we find it!"

Then Mervikk went marching across the sand, checking for clawprints. Heading towards the rocks round the edge of the lagoon.

I bent down. I had spotted a seagoblin shell — but it was empty. No seagoblin living inside it right now. I held it to my ear. Listened to the faint chatter of the last seagoblin to live in it.

Then I put it back. Ready for another little seagoblin to move in. Maybe even two, doing a shellshare – as the shell was quite big.

Then I heard a shout from Mervikk. "Flo!" he shouted. "FLO! *Quick!* Look! LOOK what I found!" He was jumping up and down, beckoning me over, and pointing behind a big rock, looking thrilled.

Then he disappeared behind it.

I ran. Had he *found* it? The MUTANT? Had he actually found it?

I skidded round the rock.

I stopped. Stared.

No. Mervikk HADN'T found the mutant. He'd found an egg. A big blue egg. Completely round, the size of a gripball – and about to hatch.

Mervikk was crouched down, watching it crack open. "Look," he breathed. "Here it comes!"

Something was scrabbling its way out of the egg. First one small yellow flipper appeared. Then another. Then the top of a head. With a big tuft of yellow hair.

Oh no. Oh no NO…

"Mervikk!" I said, grabbing his arm. "Get up. Quick! Get away!"

Too late.

The egg split right open, and the whole head appeared. A small fluffy blue head with round blue eyes.

The round blue eyes of a baby woddelflomp.

Staring. Staring and staring up at Mervikk – the very first thing it saw…

✶

"Me?" said Mervikk, eyes popping as he stared at the woddelflomp chick, cheeping up at him. "ME? This baby, this woddelflomp … it thinks I'm its *dad*? Because I'm the first thing it SAW?"

"Yes," I said.

Because I know about woddelflomp chicks. I saw it on *Wild and Wonderful Witchglobe.*

The mum lays the egg – then abandons it. Then the dad sits on the egg until it hatches. But every so often the dad has to leave to find food. And if the egg hatches while the dad is away – like now – the chick attaches itself to the first thing it sees…

In this case, Mervikk.

I ran and got Mum. "Mum," I said. "Something's happened. You have to come and see."

Mum did see. She stared down at the woddelflomp chick, snoozing in Mervikk's arms.

"Mervikk," she said, shaking her head. "I'm afraid you can't keep him."

Then she pointed at the sign…

TAKE NOTHING BUT PICTURES
LEAVE NOTHING BUT FOOTPRINTS

"Mum – we can't leave him here," I said. "The dad will reject him now he smells of witchkid."

Then Mervikk started panicking. "Flo's-mum," he said, clutching the chick tightly to his chest. "Please, I'm BEGGING you – please let me keep him. I'll be the best woddelflomp dad I can be. I can do it, I *can*. I understand woddelflomps. I have EXPERIENCE of being a woddelflomp. I can teach him the *ways* of woddelflomps. Please."

The chick opened his eyes. Stared up at Mum. Yawned. Then cheeped.

"Ah," said Mum, head on one side. A gooey sort of look crept across her face. Then she gave the chick a little stroke. "Ah," she said again.

Then she got to her feet, and her fingers went flying.

"*Abrakkida Rune*," she said briskly. And a shimmering magicreation began to appear. Square, and purple, with shiny silver buckles. A handbag. A LARGE handbag…

Easily large enough to smuggle a woddelflomp chick off Kraggen.

✦

The clock struck seven. It was time to light the first Witchen crown candle.

Me and Hetty stood, alone in the kitchen, staring at the Witchen crown. The glistening silver crown, hanging in the window – with five candles, all shaped like skrumpel seeds. One for each day of the skrumpel-seed planting.

The others were all gone now. Mervikk was busy taking pictures of his woddelflomp chick, asleep in a soft comfy basket. Mum and Grandma were chatting in the sitting room.

Hetty lit the first candle, the Monday candle. And we stood there, staring. At the crown, and at the flickering flame of the candle.

Hetty stared at me, her face solemn. Round her neck, a gleaming green necklace. A Witchen Day gift to Hetty from Dad – the jewel of the Valliants. Worn by Kora Valliant in the mysterious painting. Worn since by generations of first-born Valliant witches.

"Flo," said Hetty, taking hold of my hands. "Let's make our wish. Our first Witchen crown wish."

And we stood there, me and Hetty. Staring at the glow of the flickering flame.

Making our silent wish.

And I knew. Me, Hetty – our wish was the same.

For Dad to be here. To be back. Back with us for Witchen Day.

Chapter 22

Early next morning a harsh cry woke me. A screeching cry. The cry of a skragglehead in pain.

I jumped out of bed. Wherever it was – I had to help it.

I used to be *very* scared of skraggleheads. One bit me on the leg when I was small, then hurled me across the garden. It made me EXTREMELY ill.

For years after that, skraggleheads filled my nightmares. Even seeing a picture of a skragglehead sent shivers right through me. And each night Mum or Dad had to check – under my bed, in my cupboards, my wardrobe – for skraggleheads.

But then came one night that changed things. One night when Dad checked my room for skraggleheads, then came and sat on my bed.

"Flo," Dad said, smiling down at me. "Do you know how many witches were bitten by skraggleheads last year? Seventeen. Out of SIX BILLION witches."

"But *I* got bitten," I said.

"You were unlucky," Dad said. "Skraggleheads don't WANT to bite witches."

"Why *did* it bite me, then?" I said.

"Who knows?" said Dad. "Skraggleheads are intelligent, curious creatures. They have little fear. Perhaps it tried a nibble to see what you were. Then realised a witchchild is NOT a nice taste to a skragglehead."

"But that skragglehead — it hissed at me. It sounded cross," I said.

"Perhaps it had a nest nearby," said Dad. "It was the hatching season. Perhaps it thought you were going to harm its egg or its chick."

"But skraggleheads are ugly and scary," I said, teeth clattering. "And they have teeth like saws in their beaks."

"Flo," Dad said. "Those saws in a skragglehead's beak — it uses them for sifting food. If food can pass through the gaps in the saws, it is in small enough pieces to feed to its chick."

Then he smiled more. "Besides," he said. "There is balance in nature. Without skraggleheads to eat them, there would be FAR MORE scuttlepins."

"More scuttlepins?" I said, with a shiver. I was NOT fond of scuttlepins. The way I would suddenly catch sight of one. Six little legs – all purple and hairy – whizzing across the floor. Or sometimes scuttling about in my bed when I pulled back the covers.

Now Dad took my hand. "Flo," he said. "I can tell you a secret about skraggleheads. But first you have to look at this picture."

Then he showed me a picture. And I started to quake. Just looking at the scraggly feathers, the curved beak, the hooked claws. The *eyes*…

"But Daddy," I said, "those eyes – they're glaring at me. They scare me."

"Those skragglehead eyes can see for MILES," Dad said. "A skragglehead sitting on the roof of this house could see a scuttlepin down in Haggspit Harbour."

Dad smiled at me. "You can't change a skragglehead, Flo," he said. "It is what it is. But you *can* change the way that you see it."

162

Then he pointed. "And now, Flo, for the secret. See under that chin. That lighter bit of fur. Tickle a skragglehead right there – and it will go *completely* still. Into a trance. A skragglehead loves being tickled."

And, as I stared at the picture, at that skragglehead chin – something inside me *did* start to change. So here, now, I followed the harsh, screeching cry – and I ran.

It was down in the cove. Trapped. Struggling and panicking. Flapping its huge wings, snapping its huge beak. A bit of wire wrapped round one huge claw. A flapping rubbish bag wound round its leg.

It was huge. Bigger than me. And, when it saw me – it struggled even more.

I crouched down as near to it as I dared. I talked softly, talked quietly – told it again and again that I meant it no harm. And slowly, the skragglehead's struggle grew less. Until, with trembling fingers, I reached out to its chin. And started to tickle.

The skragglehead went still. Into a trance, just like Dad said. And, as gently as I could, I unwrapped the wire. Untangled the bag. Then stood up, and backed away.

The skragglehead got to its feet. Stared down at me.

I stared back. It was strange-looking, yes – but not ugly. There was beauty in that face. In the wise eyes.

Then the skragglehead bent its head – almost as if in thanks – and, with one beat of its huge strong wings, it took off. Soared into the sky and was gone.

I whooshed back up the Helter 13 and into the garden. Then I heard voices.

Mum, already out on the terrace – and with Mr Potions2Go. Both of them, at the table, open witchfixers in front of them. With a pile of toasted brikkels, and a big jug of blorberry juice. Having a breakfast meeting…

"Kristabel," Mr Potions2Go was booming, tapping away at his witchfixer. "I am *liking* what I'm hearing! I am LIKING it! An event witches will talk about for years to come. A night of fund-raising, streamed all over the witchglobe! This baby has LEGS!"

I was about to sneak round the side of the house, but I was too late – Mum had seen me.

"Flo," she said, beckoning me over. "Flo!"

I trudged over, wishing I didn't have to.

"Meristo," Mum said. "This is Flo. My younger daughter."

"Delighted," Mr Potions2Go said. And he smiled, a wide smile, all teeth, like a sawdredger.

Then he patted me on the head. "Enchanting," he said. "Quite enchanting."

But you know, don't you, as a witchkid? You know when a grown-up witch is pretending.

Just then we heard footsteps. A witch striding out to the terrace. Grandma behind her. A grown-up witch, but young, and dressed in shimmering dark green robes.

Grimmelda Hurlstruk. The daughter of Mr Potions2Go.

I knew her face from the witchscreen – but in real life, she looked harder. Taller. Her face more bony. Her mouth more thin. Her eyes more staring.

"Daddy," she said. "You're needed. It is time we left."

And her voice was soft – but hard. Like steel wrapped in silk. Then she smiled – but not a real smile. A cold sort of smile.

"Grimmelda," Mr Potions2Go said pompously, rising to his feet. "I am ALWAYS needed."

Then he snapped his witchfixer shut. "Sadly this meeting must be *concluded*, Kristabel," he said. "I have a meeting with inspectors at my Witchenfinn factory. A MOST important meeting."

Then – oh, yuk. He grabbed Mum's hand and he gave it a kiss. "Kristabel, I bid you farewell," he said. "For now… But our discussions must CONTINUE."

"Indeed," said Mum, sounding brisk and efficient. "I shall investigate, Meristo. Work on the details. Put together some ideas."

"What say a dinner date tomorrow night?" said Mr Potions2Go, smiling his toothy smile again. "To shimmy this skyrider towards lift-off? Shall we say eight o'clock? At mine?"

And off he strutted. "Grimmelda," he said. "Lead the way."

"Daddy," she said. "I shall."

Then she turned on her heel and was gone.

✦

There was a snort from Grandma. "I don't trust those Hurlstruks, Kristabel," she said. "Something SHADY about them. Not witches to do business with."

"Mother," said Mum. "Potions2Go is one of the most powerful companies on the whole witchglobe. And this is an opportunity. To team up, to create an event to remember."

Grandma snorted. "And what IS this event?" she said.

"That has yet to be finalised," said Mum. "Meristo and I shall discuss things further over dinner tomorrow night."

"Dinner? You have a *dinner* date with that RECENTLY DIVORCED witchman?" Grandma said, eyes popping. Then her eyes narrowed. "I hope you are not getting *ideas*, Kristabel," she said. "Boyfriend ideas. You with your SILLY requirements."

Mum's requirements...

She has three of them – three things she looks for in a boyfriend: money, celebrity and a strong bumpy nose.

Mum glared at Grandma. "My requirements are NOT silly," she said. "They are sensible."

Grandma snorted again. "If you mentioned requirements to Lyle Skritchett he would laugh in your face. Tell you what a *nincompoop* you are. He always DID tell you the truth, Kristabel. You just couldn't stand it."

Mum's mouth went into a thin tight line. "Mother," she hissed. "STOP."

But Grandma didn't. "You know why none of your ghastly boyfriends ever last?" she said, jabbing a finger at Mum. "Because you are STILL in love with Lyle Skritchett."

I thought Mum would shriek at Grandma – but she didn't. A whole lot of expressions flitted across her face. So fast I wasn't sure what they all were. Then Mum stuck her fingers in her ears. "Not! Listening!" she hissed. Then she got up from the table and marched inside.

And that was when I heard wings. Beating wings. And then, over the cliff top, they appeared. Not just one skragglehead – but hundreds. Beating towards me. Hundreds of huge flapping birds.

They flew overhead, the whole flock of skraggleheads. Swooping and swerving, making shapes and patterns, astonishing shapes in the sky. One beautiful swirling display. Right above me.

Then they swooped out to sea, and were gone.

Chapter 23

"THIS Gigi has to see!" Hetty shrieked, next morning. Then she snapped a Kwikpik of the woddelflomp chick, curled up in Mervikk's lap, guzzling a bottle of kronkel-milk.

"Me, a dad!" Mervikk said, beaming.

Then he stroked the chick's head gently. "Son," he said. "I am going to look after you. I am going to be a HANDS-ON dad."

Hetty was lying on the floor now, snapping a close-up. "So, what's his name, then?" she said.

Mervikk looked down at the chick, eyebrows knotting. "Son…" he said, thinking hard. "Son, you need a name. But what?"

Then his eyes lit up. "I know," he said. "Flibben, that's what I'm calling him. Flibben — after my dad. Flibben Ashbok Junior."

Flibben Ashbok Junior was yawning now. Stomach bulging with milk. Then he closed his eyes, ready to sleep again.

Hetty sat back on her heels, disappointed. "He doesn't DO much," she said.

Mervikk beamed at her. "He will, Hetty," he said. "Trust me, he will."

Because me and Mervikk checked on the witchweb about woddelflomps. And it said this:

A newly-hatched woddelflomp chick is a sleepy-head! It will sleep for most of the first thirty-six hours after hatching!

But woddelflomp chicks change day by day — much faster than witchkids! The second day after hatching, your chick will be able to run, swim and forage for food!

And woddelflomp chicks are quick learners. You can teach your chick some simple tricks, like kicking or heading a ball!

Woddelflomp chicks have an astonishing sense of smell. They can be trained – from only THREE DAYS OLD – to track a trail both on the ground, and in the air!

In the Shiverlands, witchwardens use woddelflomps to track down criminals. A woddelflomp can track a witch up to TWO HUNDRED MILES away!

Mervikk lifted Flibben gently back into his basket, and tucked the blankets around him. "Sleep well, Flibben," Mervikk said. "And I'll see you later."

After that, Mum took us to Kronebay for the day, but not before Mervikk gave Grandma a list of instructions.

"Flo's-gran," he said. "Flibben needs one bottle of kronkel-milk while we're out. But NO MORE. Because it's easy to overfeed a woddelflomp chick – and they have a tendency to *blubber*. And I have squished up some blorberries for him to try his first taste of solid food – but he might spit them out."

"Have no fear, Mervikk," said Grandma. "I am QUITE USED to dealing with fussy eaters. Kristabel was one."

We spent the morning on the beach in Kronebay – and got some useful diving tips from a merboy sunning himself on a rock. After that we had lunch – pelloligan fritters and chips on the beach. Then Mum took us to Banshees.

Banshees is the biggest shop in Kronebay. Mum stood in the entrance to the witchkid department and waved us in. "Flo, Mervikk – you may choose yourselves a holiday gift!" she said.

Mervikk chose binoculars – mutant-hunting binoculars. And I chose a book – *Wild and Wonderful Witchglobe*.

It was my kind of book. The book of the witchscreen series. Big and heavy, and full of pictures of the astonishing creatures that live on the witchglobe.

With a FUN FACTS box on every double page, like on page 8:

Gritterbacks have THREE HEARTS as well as three heads!

Splorgs poop ONCE A YEAR – and it takes ALL DAY!

Zizzwings only FLY BACKWARDS and UPSIDE DOWN!

Then we met up with Hetty, and we all went shopping for Witchen Day gifts.

Me and Hetty both bought a gift for Dad. We always do. So Dad can open them all when he's back.

And that evening, me and Hetty lit the second Witchen crown candle. Made our second Witchen crown wish – the same as the first.

Then, once again, me and Hetty stood there, watching the flickering flames – two of them now…

Hetty looked at me. "I *am* sure Dad will be back, Flo," she said, and she was biting her lip. "TOTALLY sure. Of *course* I am. It's just that … all this *waiting* … it's SO hard."

She looked at me, and her mouth turned right down. "Where *is* he, Flo?" she said. "Oh, where IS he?"

Then we heard a shriek from the sitting room. From Grandma. "Kristabel!" she shrieked. "That ghastly witchman! Your dinner date! He's about to be on *FinnNews*!"

★

Grandma was leaning right forward on the sofa, staring at *FinnNews* – which is the local witchscreen channel, as Kronebay is right near the border with Witchenfinn.

A witchhack with very straight hair and scary big

eyelashes was sitting behind a desk with a nameplate on it – Morgan de Witt.

"Earlier today," the witchhack said, "I met up with Meristo Hurlstruk, millionaire owner of the Potions2Go empire at his Witchenfinn factory – one of the biggest employers in our region. But events took a VERY unexpected turn…"

The witchscreen cut to another picture. And there she was again – Morgan de Witt, standing with Mr Potions2Go, outside his factory. And, behind them, inspectors were clambering out of a skyrider.

"So, Meristo Hurlstruk," Morgan de Witt said. "You're here today at your Potions2Go factory to meet with inspectors? To check all is as it should be in your factory?"

"Indeed I am," said Mr Potions2Go, smiling his sawdredger smile. "I shall offer the inspectors EVERY help in their investigation."

He turned. The inspectors were being greeted by a scurrying witchman. A witchman I recognised – one I'd seen scurrying around at Jasmonikka Villa.

The smile spread across Mr Potions2Go's face. "As will my assistant, Tremblikkon Stoop," he said, waving one pudgy hand at the scurrying witchman.

"So, you're confident the inspectors will find everything in order?" said Morgan de Witt.

"Absolutely," said Mr Potions2Go, nodding and puffing up his chest. "I take Witch Wellbeing and Safety issues VERY seriously indeed. As *all* us businesswitches in positions of great power should."

He paused. The sawdredger smile spread even further. "And I am just as careful with my non-business ventures, my good works," he said. "Such as my Hurlstruk Happy Homes."

Now the smile was stretching right across his face, reaching his ears. "And talking of good works," he said, "I expect to have another announcement shortly. A *most* exciting charitable venture, with one of our most popular magazines."

Grandma snorted, Mum glared at her – and *that* was when it happened. When events took the VERY unexpected turn…

✳

A unicorn, a huge unicorn, majestic and strong, white wings beating – came soaring up from behind the Potions2Go factory. Soaring through the sky.

I stared. At its long white mane, flowing in the breeze. At the sunlight glinting off its long straight horn. At its dazzling white wings beating a strong steady rhythm.

Then it landed. On the roof of the factory.

And – faster than I can snap my fingers, faster

than I can blink my eyes – the unicorn vanished.

It was gone. But now, in its place – was a witchman.

A CAPED witchman…

A MASKED witchman…

Right there – on the *roof* of the Potions2Go factory.

Chapter 24

"A semblawitch!" Grandma cackled. "That witchman – he's a SEMBLAWITCH!"

I stared. Stared more. Stared and *stared* up at the mysterious masked witchman.

Because Grandma was right. That witchman…

He *was* a semblawitch.

He HAD to be.

There was no other way he could have changed like that. Changed – in the blink of an eye – from unicorn to witchman. With no transforming spell. No drinking a potion. Nothing.

It had to be semblawitchery…

That special magiskill. That mega-magiskill. The skill of transforming into any creature – *any* living creature – in the whole of Witchworld. Of becoming that creature, of speaking its language, of BEING that creature…

The rarest of ALL magiskills. A skill SO few witches are born with.

Not one in every eight thousand, four hundred and thirty-two witches, like submawitches.

But FAR fewer.

Only three or four semblawitches are born in each CENTURY.

But still I sat there, staring and staring. Because something was happening to me. I could feel my heart pumping faster and faster. Could feel every bit of me trembling. Tingling.

That witchman – the way he stood there, so tall, so straight…

He SO reminded me of Dad.

But… *But…*

No.

He couldn't be Dad. He could *not* be Dad.

Dad was NOT a semblawitch.

And now, as I stared, the masked witchman pointed his spellstick. And a magicreation began to appear. A shimmering magicreation.

One … two … three … four shapes.

Creatures. Short squat creatures, on sturdy legs. Creatures with squashy faces. With hair — thick as mops, thick as broomstick bristles — sticking out round their heads. With coarse fat tails swishing out behind them.

Forest trolls…

Grunting, dribbling forest trolls, with big heads and small brains.

Trolls who love money, love shiny silver coins. Not to use — but to collect. To hoard.

Trolls who can be taught to do simple tasks. All the messy, mucky jobs — all the jobs witches don't want to do.

Trolls who will work ALL DAY LONG for one shiny silver coin.

But this magicreation, these forest trolls — they were all holding banners…

CRUELTY TO TROLLS!
MAKE YOUR POTION PIPES WIDER!
INSPECTORS – CHECK THE PIPE WIDTHS!
NARROW PIPES SAVE MONEY BUT
HURT US!

Then — once again — the mysterious masked

witchman pointed his spellstick…

Straight at Mr Potions2Go.

Lines of magic swirled around his astonished head. A shimmering magicreation appeared all around him. Lots of pipes. Big bendy pipes. A tangle of pipes, twisting in all directions. See-through pipes…

I knew what they were. Ready-potions pipes. Like the ones we saw in the Witchcitizenship Awards assembly.

But these pipes were NOT gushing with potions. They were dripping with slime and rubbish and mucky potion remains.

And Mr Potions2Go was trapped inside. Squashed in one of the pipes right in the middle. Completely STUCK.

"Help!" he roared, standing there, eyes popping. "*Stop* this! What's happening? Security! SECURITY!"

And now hair – a bristling mop of hair – burst out all around his gaping face. Then a tail – a fat stubby tail of thick coarse hair – burst out of the back of his robes. Forest troll hair…

A forest troll tail…

Mr Potions2Go clutched at his hair. He clutched at his tail. He struggled. He squirmed. He roared with fury.

"Let me OUT!" he bellowed. "LET ME OUT!"

But the masked witchman stood there, up on the roof. Just stood there, arms folded, watching and waiting.

And now, on the ground – a crowd was gathering. Running from all corners of the factory. Gaping, astonished, with wide, shocked eyes at Mr Potions2Go – stuck, and with only one way to get UNSTUCK…

By wriggling. By squirming. By squeezing. By squashing his way – inch by inch – along the narrow potions pipe until he found a way out.

And, as he wriggled and squirmed and squeezed his way through – his bristling head of hair cleared the pipe ahead of him. And his short swishing tail cleared the pipe behind him…

Just as the forest trolls did every day.

And, all the while, up on the roof – the caped and masked witchman stood there watching.

Then – at last – Mr Potions2Go squeezed his way out. He staggered to his feet, dripping with slime and muck.

"*Security!*" he roared. "Where is SECURITY? *Seize* him!"

But then – the witchman was gone. In his place, a huge hairy scuttlepin, spinning a web from the roof to the ground. Until it landed. And came scuttling towards Mr Potions2Go.

Mr Potions2Go charged. "I shall CRUSH you!" he bellowed. "I shall STAMP you underfoot!"

But then – the scuttlepin was gone. And a snippersnapper – pincers waggling – started nipping at Mr Potions2Go's ankles.

"Ow! *Ow!* OW!" Mr Potions2Go bellowed, spitting with rage, hopping and clutching at his ankles.

Then the snippersnapper was gone – and a striped serpent slithered and coiled its way round Mr Potions2Go's legs.

Mr Potions2Go tripped. He went sprawling to the ground. And then – the serpent too was gone. Transformed. Back into the unicorn. That huge flying unicorn.

And I stared at the witchscreen. As, once again, that dazzling white unicorn soared up and away, into the sky.

Then was gone.

Chapter 25

"Nocturnals!" said Mervikk that evening, getting out his binoculars. "There could be nocturnal mutants, Flo. Night-time creatures!"

He beamed. "Because, if there's a mutant nibbet *and* a mutant something-else – the mutant that attacked the broomstick, there could be a mutant ANYTHING! Including nocturnals!"

Well, I wasn't sure a mutant actually *did* attack the broomstick – but I DO like being in my treehouse. It's high up in a latchenboll tree. Tucked away in its thick branches, camouflaged by its big silver leaves.

Dad made the treehouse years ago. From the ground you can hardly see it. But from inside – you can see out, all over the garden. Because Dad cut circles in all the walls. Spyholes…

Mervikk crouched down, right by a spyhole. He hung his binoculars round his neck. "I am *ready!*" he said. "If there's a mutant nocturnal about, I'll SPOT it!"

Then he put a finger to his lips. "We have to be quiet, Flo. So the nocturnals don't know we're here."

I crouched down too, listening to the chirruppellas chirruping in the grass, watching long shadows creeping across the garden. And thinking…

About that masked witchman…

About Dad…

That witchman, he SO reminded me of Dad. And that protest – it was just the sort of thing Dad would do.

But that witchman *couldn't* be Dad. No.

You were either born a semblawitch or you weren't. And Dad *wasn't.*

Then – "Stoop! STOOP!" a voice bellowed out. A voice up in next-door's garden. "Where *are* you? And where are my Yumyums?"

I peeked out through one of the spyholes. A spyhole that had looked out over wild land when

Dad built the treehouse. But not any more. Not since Jasmonikka Villa was built. Now the spyhole looks straight down into its garden. Down on to the west terrace. The one that gets the last light of the evening suns.

And here he came – Mr Potions2Go. Striding down the steps from the house, towards the terrace. He flung himself down into a big outdoor armchair, teeth grinding. He did NOT look happy.

Now a witchman came running down the steps. A small, scurrying witchman, with a nervous, twitching face. Carrying a big bowl of Yumyums.

"He humiliated me, Stoop!" Mr Potions2Go bawled. "That witchman. He HUMILIATED me. Made me a laughing stock!"

Big squirts of smoke started puffing out of his ears. "So – those pipes are a TEENY bit narrower than they should be," Mr Potions2Go bawled. "So what? Who cares? Who *cares* about forest trolls? Who cares if they get a bit squished and squashed in the pipes? NOT ME! Small pipes save money! Lovely *money*!"

Now Mr Potions2Go started gnashing his teeth. "Those inspectors – they *never* notice. We got away with it for YEARS, Stoop! But this time – they checked! Declared them *illegal*! And whose fault is THAT? The fault of that PESKY PROTESTER!"

Now smoke was pouring out of his ears in a long steady stream. "All businesswitches cut corners to save money," Mr Potions2Go bellowed. "All of us!"

Tremblikkon Stoop gave a twitch. "Erm... *Not* Aggratikka Thropistikkan," he said nervously.

"Well, she SHOULD cut corners, Stoop!" bellowed Mr Potions2Go. "She's a SILLY businesswitch. Doing everything the way she's supposed to. Obeying the law! SHAME on her!"

Now Tremblikkon Stoop spoke, shifting from foot to foot. Looking nervous. "Sir... As you know, all the pipes have to be replaced," he said. "And that means replacing every imm the pipes run to."

"I KNOW that!" bawled Mr Potions2Go. "Why are you telling me that? That pesky protester! He is trying to RUIN me!"

"Sir," said Tremblikkon Stoop. "The new imms are on their way. They will be at the factory in two days' time."

He paused, then gulped – and I could see, he was quaking. For some reason, he was actually *quaking*.

"That means, Sir," he said, quaking more, "that we must err ... *remove* the old imms."

"Yes, yes, YES! Remove them," bellowed Mr

Potions2Go. "REMOVE the old imms! Take care of it. I pay you enough. You *know* what to do! You *know* where to take them!"

"But, Sir," said Stoop – and now I could hear panic in his voice. "Should we? Are you *sure*? The report…"

"No BUTS, Stoop!" roared Mr Potions2Go. "One silly report – it means *nothing*!"

"But, Sir…" Tremblikkon Stoop was mopping his forehead and biting his lip. "Perhaps … this time, we should—"

"This time we should *what*?" said a soft silky voice.

Grimmelda Hurlstruk. Coming down the steps to the west terrace. Dressed in robes of shimmering black.

Tremblikkon Stoop quaked even more. "I just… It's just… I thought…" he stuttered.

Grimmelda Hurlstruk smiled her cold hard smile. "Perhaps Stoop," she said, softly, "it is best you do NOT think."

She stood, staring, at Tremblikkon Stoop. "And now, Stoop –" she said, staring harder, "you may go."

Tremblikkon Stoop *did* go. He scurried away, as fast as he could.

Then Grimmelda turned to Mr Potions2Go.

"Daddy," she said. "It's time to dress for dinner."

"What's for dinner, Grimmelda?" said Mr Potions2Go eagerly, rubbing his hands. "Is it lovely? Is it hot and spicy? Are there chips? What did you order?"

"Steamed larbinspike, with a mixed purple salad," said Grimmelda.

"Noooo!" Mr Potions2Go grumbled. "Not stinky old larbinspike. Daddy hates fish. And salad."

He started looking sulky. Stuck his bottom lip out. "Does Daddy HAVE to eat the salad, Grimmelda?" he said, scuffing his foot.

"Yes," she said, picking up the bowl of Yumyums. "You're too fat, Daddy. And too greedy."

Then she turned and walked back up the steps. And, heaving one big heavy sigh, Mr Potions2Go stomped up the garden behind her.

Then me and Mervikk heard something. The beating of tiny wings. And a big flutter of Witchenlands fairies – about thirty or so – landed in the garden.

★

Now, I am NOT a fan of Witchenlands fairies.

They spend most of their time admiring themselves in dewdrops. When they're not doing that they're squabbling with each other. And at dusk – they always do fairy dancing.

Like now.

They started doing the usual sort of fairy dancing. Dancing in a ring – all dainty little steps, twirling and skipping, and pointing their toes, and making little pouty faces.

I wasn't much interested. But then one of the fairies missed her footing and let out a big squeal – well, big for a fairy…

Now the squealer was tottering about, all off-balance. About to fall over. That does happen sometimes – because I once saw a TOTAL pile-up in my back garden in Haggspit. One fairy in the flutter – with two flat feet and *no* sense of rhythm – got all her steps muddled, then tripped. She fell sideways, and sent the whole fairy ring tumbling over. One after another, knocked down like dominoes. Until not one fairy was left standing.

But here, now – something happened I have NEVER seen happen before.

Because, as the squealer tripped, she collided with another fairy – a very tiny one, in a multi-coloured frock. Knocked the tiny fairy right over.

And the tiny fairy was NOT happy.

She sprawled on the ground – then picked herself

up, eyebrows knotted tight together. She started wagging her finger. Chattering, and gnashing her teeth, right in the face of the squealer. Furious with rage.

And then – her eyes began to *glow*. Actually GLOW. A bright and dazzling *green*…

I felt my mouth drop open in shock. And so did Mervikk's. Because now the fairy's whole face was changing. She started sprouting *fangs*. And *whiskers*, long bristling ones.

Then *fur* – multicoloured fur – started sprouting all over her small fairy body. And that body, those wings – they started to *grow*. To grow and grow and GROW. Then, bursting out of the fairy's head – came two waggling antlers.

Waggling ORANGE antlers…

The flutter scattered. Squealing with panic, they took to the skies. Flew across the garden, and straight out to sea.

And the creature – the HUGE creature, antlers waggling – went chasing right after them, as fast as it could.

Chapter 26

Mervikk turned towards me, eyes goggling. "That was the creature that attacked the broomstick!" he said. "It WAS a mutant! A mutant *fairy*!"

His eyes were shining. He grabbed my arm. "Flo, we are discoverers of the very first mutant IN THE WILD!" he said. "We'll be *famous*! Be in the record books! Be all over the witchweb! Invited on chat shows! And Dad – he'll be SO proud of me!"

"Mervikk," I said. "There's just one problem. We have no *proof* of the mutant."

Mervikk gaped at me. "A picture, Flo!" he groaned, slapping his forehead. "We should have got a picture!"

Then his shoulders slumped. "Call ourselves mutant hunters?" he said, gloomily. "We forgot to do the most BASIC thing. Get a picture! And no one will believe us, two witchkids saying we saw a mutant fairy. And now – now – we've missed our chance – probably FOREVER. And—"

"Mervikk, shush," I said. "There's still a chance of getting that picture. I have a *plan*."

Because I had just spotted something. Something small and pink and glittery, lying in the grass. A little fairy ribbon. One that must have fallen from the hair of a panicking fairy.

"Follow me!" I said. Then I headed down from the treehouse and across to the shed full of gardening imms.

Now – I want to say something here.

That maybe me and Mervikk should have thought a bit more about that conversation we just overheard. About Tremblikkon Stoop, and what he said. About Mr Potions2Go, and what *he* said…

And that maybe some of you witchkids – *way* smarter than me and Mervikk were right then – are doing just that.

We were NOT.

We forgot *all* about that conversation. We were FAR too busy thinking about the mutant fairy – and about my plan…

✦

"So, let me get this right," said Mervikk, sitting on the shed bench. "First we train Flibben to *track*."

"Yes," I said. "Starting tomorrow, using all the training tips on page seventy-five of *Wild and Wonderful Witchglobe*. Then, on Friday – he can track the fairy the ribbon belonged to!"

"Genius," said Mervikk. Then he frowned. "But what then? When we find the nest?"

"We AMBUSH the fairies!" I said. "And make them CROSS!"

Then I brandished the little spraysquirter imm. "With this!" I said. "We set it to go whizzing all around the nest. Get it to soak all the fairies!"

I know, I *know*. It's mean to soak a fairy.

But we had to make them cross – and soaking them was the best way I could think of. Because fairies are *very* fussy about their hair. They HATE getting it wet.

"Being soaked by the spraysquirter is BOUND to set off the mutant," I said. "Then – click – we get some Kwikpiks. Lots of them. *Proof!* Mutant proof!"

Mervikk was beaming. "Brilliant," he said. "Dad will be AMAZED when he sees the Kwikpiks! And not just dad. Witchboffins too – they need to see the Kwikpiks. See there's a mutant fairy about!"

Just then Hetty called from inside the house. It was time to light the third Witchen crown candle.

Straight after me and Hetty had made our third Witchen crown wish, Hetty dragged me off to her room.

She pointed at two outfits laid out on her bed. Stared at them, head on one side. "The witchfliks tonight, Flo…" she said. "Should I wear that … or that? Which is more likely to make Errken *seethe* with jealousy?"

"I don't know," I said. "But … Hetty. Is it a good idea – trying to make Errken jealous? Is that the right thing to do?"

Hetty's eyebrows shot up. "It totally is, Flo," she said, nodding hard.

"But … he did choose to date Veracity," I said. "So … is it fair? To him? To her? And what about Archie? Is it fair – using him to make Errken jealous?"

Hetty did her tinkling laugh. Patted me on the head. "You know *so* little," she said – which she often does. "Now, go – witchteen busy!"

But I didn't go, not yet. Because I had something to ask her.

"Hetty," I said, "that masked witchman. Did he … *remind* you of anyone?"

Hetty went totally still. "No," she said, in a stiff sort of voice. "No one at all."

I knew she was lying.

Because Hetty may be a brilliant witchteen liar, but NOT this time. I knew, as if she had said it out loud, that he DID remind her of someone…

Dad.

And I also knew she was NOT happy about it. But, still – I had one more thing to say.

"That masked witchman, Hetty…" I said, "he was protesting about trolls. *Trolls.*"

Now Hetty's eyebrows knotted right together. "*Forest* trolls," she hissed. "NOT snow trolls."

Then she pushed me towards the door. "Now go. GO!"

I *did* go.

I went to see Mum. All dressed up for her dinner date with Mr Potions2Go. I had something I wanted to ask *her*.

"Mum," I said, standing in her doorway. "Do you think it is *ever* possible for a witch to BECOME a semblawitch, not be born one? Is there *any* chance? Any chance AT ALL?"

Mum looked at me. "No," she said, in a small quiet voice. "No chance at all."

"It's just … that masked witchman…" I said, "what he did – it was just the sort of thing that … that, well – *Dad* would do."

Mum looked at me more. "Flo," she said, a sad look in her eyes. "I would give anything in the world for you to be right. *Anything*. But you're not."

Then she blew her nose – HARD. And walked briskly out of her bedroom and towards the stairs – just as a huge thunderclap boomed out. The front door burst open, and a small parcel flew into the hallway.

A Thunderbolt Delivery for Mervikk.

✦

"Look, Flibben," said Mervikk, beaming. "Look what me and Flo's-mum got you! Your very own collar!"

He put the collar round Flibben's neck. And Flibben stood, puffing his chest out – looking proud as a yafflepeck.

Dangling off the collar, twinkling and shining, was a small silver disc with writing engraved on it. A nametag: FLIBBEN ASHBOK JUNIOR

"Dad!" Mervikk beamed. "This evening – at LAST – I am screenchatting Dad."

He checked his watch. "In less than one hour," he said. "And there's SO much to tell him!"

But the hour passed, and Mervikk never *did* get to screenchat with his Dad. Or to tell him all his news. Because when Mervikk called the medicentre, a witchmedic said his dad was worse. All of a sudden, much worse.

Mervikk's mouth turned right down when he heard. "Dad's got Complications," he said, looking glum. "And I hate it when Dad gets Complications. He can't speak, he can't hold things, he can't do *anything*. And Complications go on and on and ON. Complications mean *months* more of Dad being sick."

Then Mervikk sighed. "It's not that I mind looking after Dad," he said. "I don't mind. Not at all – Dad is my whole family. My *only* family. And I WANT to look after him. Because there's no one else who can. No cousins. No uncles, no aunties. No one. It's just me and Dad."

Then Mervikk gave an even bigger sigh. "It's just – I really REALLY wish Dad was well," he said. "But he won't be. Not ever. There's no cure for Stumbles."

"Mervikk," said Grandma briskly, patting his hand, "there is a cure for *everything* – including Stumbles. Witchboffins just haven't found it yet. But witchboffins WILL. And then, your father will be cured."

"I hope so, Flo's-gran," Mervikk said. "I hope so."

But that night, I heard sniffs. Then mutters. Then sobs, small quiet sobs. All coming from Mervikk's bedroom. And I knew. Those small quiet sobs – they were all because of his dad.

I was shocked.

Because some witchkids cry a lot – but NOT Mervikk. Mervikk is always smiling. Always happy. Never complaining.

And I realised then how brave Mervikk was. About his dad being ill. About being his carer. About everything.

So I went into his room to try and cheer him up.

But Mervikk was asleep. Sniffing and muttering and sobbing – but fast asleep.

Chapter 27

Back in my room, the lantern flickered in my window. I lay there, listening to the small quiet sobs from Mervikk, and thinking about Dad...

My dad.

Remembering that last Witchen Day at Kronebay. Me and Dad, going out into the garden. Me dressed as Destiny Daggett. Dad, swirling behind me, wearing a tablecloth around his shoulders.

Remembering what he said...

"A cape!" Dad said, twirling round in his tablecloth. "Every crimefighter MUST have a cape."

Then, from his robe pocket, he took out a mask –

made from black paper.

"And every crimefighter, Flo," Dad said, fixing the mask over his eyes, "must make sure to go INCOGNITO."

"Incognito?" I said.

"He must conceal his true identity," Dad said. "Just as Destiny Daggett does."

Remembering more…

Me, sitting with Dad, watching *Wild and Wonderful Witchglobe*. Watching a vast flock of unicorns flying across the witchscreen.

"Imagine, Flo," Dad said, eyes shining, "being a semblawitch! Being that creature – no doppel potion, no spell. Speaking the language of the unicorns as they fly. Knowing – really knowing – how it feels to be one of those strange and mysterious creatures."

Then Dad smiled at me. "For of all the great magiskills us witches may be gifted, semblawitchery – THAT is the greatest."

But Dad was *not* a semblawitch.

All the same – that night, I dreamt about Dad.

I dreamt he was here. *Here*. Right NOW. And I woke with a longing so fierce, so strong – it made me ache all over. Ache from the top of my head to the soles of my feet…

Then – I heard something.

The sound of pounding feet. Huge pounding feet. Somewhere outside.

I leapt to my window. And there – running across our garden in three big bounds, leaping off the cliff, and down towards the cove – was the *Trigoggladron*.

✦

"Mervikk, wake up!" I said. "WAKE UP!"

Mervikk rolled over, hair sticking up on end, face groggy. "Wassup?" he said.

"The Trigoggladron!" I said. "It's here! In the cove!"

NOW Mervikk was awake. He leapt out of bed, eyes popping. Then we both ran downstairs, grabbed Grandma's cake tin – ready at all times, just in case – and hurtled out into the garden and towards the Helter 13.

Down in the cove, we crept. Towards the huge rocks. Towards the huge cave at the end. We crept, thrilled. Trembling.

This was our chance. Mine and Mervikk's. Our chance to ask questions. Questions we SO wanted the answers to.

Feelings lurched through me. Thrilling feelings. Feelings of hope. Feelings that maybe now – NOW – I could find out where Dad was.

But other feelings too. Feelings that set my teeth

clacking and my knees knocking. Feelings of fear. Of TERROR.

Thinking of the book, of *Magical Myths*. Knowing every word, almost by heart. Knowing what it said about the Trigoggladron. About those three snarling heads of the huge dribbling ogre…

The first of those heads – the hungry head, it must be fed. The second of those heads – the grumpy head, it must be soothed by sweet music. Only then will the third head – the head of all knowledge, answer your three questions…

But know this, witchchildren, know this. If the hungry head is not fed to its liking, if the grumpy head is not soothed by the sounds – then…

BEWARE.

For the Trigoggladron will NOT answer your questions – not the first, not the second, not the third. Instead, the Trigoggladron will gather you up in its huge bristling paws. And that head – that third head, so full of knowledge – it knows of WAYS…

Ways to DISPOSE of a witchchild.

One thousand, two hundred and thirty-seven ways.

And each of those ways, every one of those ways - is TOO GHASTLY, TOO GRUESOME to tell in our tale...

We were here. Outside the cave.

We could hear muttering from inside. A low booming voice, muttering to itself — just like Mervikk did when he was fast asleep.

I gulped. And, beside me, Mervikk did too.

Was the Trigoggladron sleeping? Was it lying there, in the cave, all sprawled out? Those three ogre heads all muttering and dribbling?

And if it was asleep — should we wake it? How *did* you wake the Trigoggladron? And if we woke it, would that make the grumpy head *extra* grumpy — even harder to please?

I gulped more. How could I sing to that grumpy ogre head? Sing when my mouth was so dry I could hardly *swallow*?

I had to sing. Just HAD to.

On trembling legs, I stepped into the cave, Mervikk beside me.

And there it was... The Trigoggladron.

I gaped. So did Mervikk.

Because the *Magical Myths* were ALL wrong.

Yes – the Trigoggladron had three huge heads. And yes – they were dribbling, and gap-toothed, and ugly, with hair piled up in huge tangled knots.

But the Trigoggladron was NOT an ogre. She was an ogress – a lady ogre. Busy knitting herself a vast pink scarf.

And the three heads – they all had big stretchy smiles.

"Visitors! How LOVELY!" boomed the Trigoggladron, looking thrilled to see us. Then she put her knitting down and clapped two hands the size of dustbin lids.

"Greetings, witchchildren!" the three heads boomed out, all six bulging eyes shining with happiness.

And I remembered what Mr Prankett said. That these stories, the *Magical Myths*, were told by the cave witches, sitting around their fires. Handed down from one generation to the next. Details changing along the way.

Now Mervikk stepped forward, eyes popping, and held out the cake. "I hope you enjoy this," he said, with a tiny wobble in his voice.

"Ooh, cake!" boomed the left-hand head. Then

the Trigoggladron clapped her two hands again – and the sound made my ears ring.

She leaned forward, licking her plump pink lips. "Goody," she said eagerly. "Cake! CAKE! Yummy yummy blorberry cake!"

✦

Nothing was like *Magical Myths* said it would be. The Trigoggladron wasn't mean or grumpy. Not even very scary. And she LOVED the cake. Thanked Mervikk again and again for bringing it.

Then, as soon as I started singing, the huge musical head started nodding and swaying, right on to the end.

And, as I finished – the middle head looked delighted. "Lovely," it boomed. "Enchanting! So ask away, witchchildren! Ask away!"

"You first," I whispered to Mervikk, and he stepped forward.

"Please, Trigoggladron," he said, eagerly – but very VERY politely. "Could you tell me the cure for Stumbles?"

"Ooh, Stumbles… Let me think… Stumbles…" the Trigoggladron said, frowning hard and scratching her huge dribbling middle head. Then her plump lips opened in a huge, wide smile. "Ah-ha! I *have* it, I have it!" she said.

And she told us.

Mervikk stood there, eyes shining. The cure – he had the CURE for Stumbles! And we had it on film, recorded on his skychatter.

Then it was my turn. I stepped forward, quickly as I could. Every bit of me trembling. Now… NOW I was going to find out about Dad. Where he was.

"My question is this," I said – and I could hardly speak, hardly breathe for excitement.

Six bushy eyebrows shot up at once.

"*Your* question?" the Trigoggladron said. And all three heads started tutting, and staring at each other, eyebrows knotted, foreheads furrowed.

I felt my insides lurch.

Then – "One question only," the middle head boomed, with a frown.

"But…" I stammered. "The book… *Magical Myths*… It said three."

"Three?" boomed the middle head, looking astonished. Then all three huge heads started shaking. "This book – whatever this book *is* – is TOTALLY wrong. One question only. And once I have answered it, I vanish. Like this…"

Then—

POOF!

She was gone.

Chapter 28

"Flo," said Mervikk. "We'll train Flibben, just like you planned – then we'll track that Trigoggladron down. Track her from the cave."

"Thanks, Mervikk," I said. "But the tide's coming in. The cave's already half full of water. I don't think there'll be a trail to track."

Then I tried to smile – but it was hard. If only … if *only* I could have asked the Trigoggladron my question. Now I would know, I would HAVE the answer.

I had been so close. SO close to finding Dad.

But knowing that – knowing how close I had

been — it made me feel worse.

Grandma patted my hand. "Flo," she said briskly, "if we have found the Trigoggladron once, we shall find her *again*. In the meantime, our search for the grimbleshank plant begins."

Because Grandma had looked at Mervikk's skychatter footage. The recipe to make a potion to cure Stumbles. But just one ingredient made her frown.

"Seeds from the grimbleshank plant," she said. "A plant I have never heard of. It must be RARE. We shall check the E list."

The E list … full of information about every known creature, every tree, every plant in Witchworld. Including its E status: Entirely New, Existing, Endangered, Extinct.

We checked the E list. And the first message on screen was this…

GRIMBLESHANK PLANT
Native to the Wild Isles
E status: EXTINCT

Mervikk slumped. "Oh no," he said. "Not *extinct*? It CAN'T be."

"Extinct?" snorted Grandma. "Mervikk, ghouls

were extinct, according to the E list. And doppels too."

Mum patted Mervikk's hand. "Mervikk," she said, "for once, I am in agreement with my mother. Extinct merely means no witches have seen it for some years."

Then she got out her skychatter. "I shall get on to it at once," she said, and swirled out of the room.

Ten minutes later, she came back, talking into her skychatter. "Yes," she said. "Yes. Thank you. I am most grateful."

"Mervikk," she beamed. "I have found a plant hunter! An *expert*! The finest in the whole of United Witchenlands. A government adviser! And − by a truly ASTONISHING piece of luck − he is here! Here in Kronebay! Investigating an outbreak of Blotch in seaweed. He will be with us shortly."

And fifteen minutes later, there was a brisk *rat tat tat* at the front door.

Me and Mervikk ran to open it. Grandma beside us.

A witchman was standing there. One I recognised. Gilbert Grittokk.

Grandma gaped. So did Gilbert. Both their mouths dropped open. I could see thoughts flitting through their heads one after another. But then—

"Gilbert," said Grandma, pursing up her mouth. "Some things are too important for petty arguments to get in the way. Let us work together — however inexcusable your behaviour."

"*My* behaviour?" said Gilbert, eyes popping. "Dorabel Skritchett, it was YOU who behaved badly. ABYSMALLY!"

Grandma's eyebrows shot up. "I most certainly did NOT behave abysmally," she snorted. "The only abysmal behaviour that day was yours, Gilbert! YOURS!"

I'd heard enough. So I jumped between the two of them.

"Excuse me," I said. "But I am well over SEVENTY years younger than BOTH of you. And *I* can see that you are behaving like a pair of witchtoddlers. How come you can't?"

I didn't budge. I stood there, staring from one to the other, arms folded. Waiting.

Grandma started to scuff her foot. "Gilbert," she said. "Shall we put our past quarrels behind us? Once and for all?"

"Dorabel," said Gilbert, looking at me a little sheepishly. "I will if you will."

"So, Dorabel," said Gilbert, "the grimbleshank

210

plant… Last sighted forty-nine years ago. Never since."

Then he opened his backpack and got out a teapot. A small ugly teapot in the shape of a goblin.

"Gilbert," said Grandma, eyes popping. "Is that what I think it is?"

"Dorabel," said Gilbert. "It is."

I knew what it was too. I've seen one before. Grandma has one. A magic mirror. Banned for the last twenty years…

Grandma started looking jealous. "How come you're allowed one and I'm not?" she said. "I'm a government adviser too. *I* should be allowed one."

"Allowed one?" said Gilbert, eyebrows shooting up. "I am absolutely *not* allowed one, Dorabel. NO witches are allowed magic mirrors. All magic mirrors MUST be handed in to the government. No exceptions."

Then he and Grandma cackled.

Gilbert's magic mirror worked just like Grandma's. The goblin teapot started to glow silver, then sort of … *melted*. Melted into swirling silver rivers – not quite liquid, not quite solid. Rivers that went dripping and pooling across the sitting room wall – until it was one huge shimmering wall of silver mirror.

"I'll set it to Roaming," Gilbert said. "Narrow it down, Dorabel. That is the key. Finding the most LIKELY islands for a so-called *extinct* grimbleshank plant to be!"

Then he waved his hands – and hundreds of tiny pictures appeared in the mirror. Every single one of the Wild Isles.

Then Gilbert spoke loudly and clearly. "Magic mirror," he said. "Show me the islands with thick, shade-giving trees."

Immediately – some of the islands were gone.

"Magic mirror," Gilbert said next. "Show me the islands with plenty of fresh water."

More islands were gone.

On and on Gilbert went. And each time, more and more islands were gone.

Until, ten questions later – there were just three. Three rocky islands, much bigger and clearer. Each taking up one-third of the mirror.

Gilbert zoomed in on one. Then started shaking his head. "See that plant there," he said, pointing. "Boriskulloris aspikkalormin. So the soil is *very* acid. Too acid for the grimbleshank plant."

Which left only two islands. Even bigger. Even clearer.

And that was when the feelings started. Tiny

feelings. Horrible feelings. Feelings I knew...

"Ah-ha!" said Gilbert, leaning forward. "This one, Dorabel. This one looks promising! The right sort of terrain, and plenty of water."

He waved his hand, and the mirror zoomed in. And now, just one island filled the screen. One island stretched out across it. Clear as clear.

A tall, craggy island. Lots of cliffs, lots of hills, lots of thick twisted trees...

"Yes! Yes!" said Gilbert, as the mirror zoomed from place to place. "Askidron kempblott! Memirillium spondulikka! *Very* similar to the grimbleshank plant!"

On and on the mirror zoomed. Darting around, showing parts of the island – one after another after another...

Paths. Forests. Craggy cliffs. A river. A lagoon…

And now – as I sat there, staring at the mirror, staring at the island – those horrible feelings were growing. Those horrible, horrible feelings…

Feelings I recognised.

Shudders.

Shudders that went creeping right through me.

"Grandma," I said. "Grandma…"

And now – as the magic mirror roamed, backwards and forwards, all over the island – things were starting to flash right in front of my eyes.

Glimpses. Scenes. Snapshots. Faint shapes – but a blur, a jumble. The ground – from way up high. Cliffs. A river. A big shadowy shape – perhaps a tree? They all went swirling by. All gone in seconds. Gone too fast for me to see what they were.

And sounds, lots of sounds. Babbling, rumbling, roaring sounds… Squeals and howls and faint harsh cries. And – was that feet? Pounding feet? Was that screams?

It was too hard to say. Too muffled to hear.

And *still* the images came. Blurred glimpses.

Of lights and explosions and flames. And wings. *Wings*. HUGE flapping wings. A long snarling snout…

Then – BAM – I fell to the ground.

Chapter 29

Grandma and Mervikk picked me up off the floor. Sat me down with my back to the magic mirror.

Gilbert looked at me, gaping. "What just happened?" he said.

"The Shudders," said Mervikk proudly. "Flo is a Shudderer!"

Because all witchkids in my class know about me and Shuddering. I Shuddered once on a class trip in Haggspit – right in front of the statue of the Haggfiend.

"Shuddering, Gilbert," said Grandma, eyes gleaming, "is a Skritchett gift. Handed down to Flo from my mother. Mummy could stand on a spot, and Shudder – see witchhistory that happened there, right in front of her eyes. And now, Flo too, has the great gift of Shuddering."

I felt grumpy. I always do when I've Shuddered. I do NOT like the great gift of Shuddering – my Shudders show scary things. First, the ghoul attack. Second, the Haggfiend attack.

Not past, but future witchhistory. *My* future…

Or, at least – they had so far.

But these Shudders, I had NO idea what they showed.

Now Grandma was looking at me, eyes gleaming. "But, Flo, how INTRIGUING," she said. "You Shuddered at an *image* – an image in a magic mirror, just as Mummy once did!"

"Those Shudders, Grandma," I said, "they weren't like the others. They were fainter. MUCH fainter. A blur. A jumble. Nothing that made sense."

Grandma was nodding. "Mummy was just the same," she said. "Her magic mirror Shudders were VERY unclear – and gone in a flash. She never *did* work out what it was that she saw."

Well, nor could I.

Now Grandma frowned. "But how strange you Shuddered just then," she said. "You are not going out to that Wild Isle, you are not in fear of attack, not seeing your future witchhistory – so what *was* it you saw, I wonder?"

"I'm not sure…" I said. "I *think* I saw wings. Big flapping wings. And lots of lights, and flames. And I heard running feet. Witches' feet."

But did I? Were those witches' feet running? I just didn't know.

Grandma was thrilled. "Witches' feet!" she said. "Perhaps Gilbert's and mine! Perhaps your Shudders show not just your future, Flo, but the future of *others*! Or perhaps those feet belong to witches from the *past*! From days when witches roamed the Wild Isles. Perhaps you are a *two-way* Shudderer! Able to see both future witchhistory, and past!"

Just then, there was a loud thunderclap, the front door banged open – and an envelope flew into the sitting room.

It had writing on it…

THUNDERBOLT DELIVERY

GILBERT GRITTOKK

It also had the Hovelhagg coat of arms on the

front. Official government business.

Gilbert ripped it open. "My application form," he said. "For clearance. To get the Shimmering turned off. To visit that Wild Isle."

Then he flipped through it and groaned. "Twenty-seven pages long," he said, glumly.

"Twenty-seven pages?" said Grandma, eyes popping.

"Clearance is a tricky thing, Dorabel," Gilbert said, heaving a big sigh. "I'll need evidence – that it's possible the grimbleshank plant still grows there, film of the Trigoggladron, all sorts of evidence. I'll need references to vouch for my good character. I'll need—"

"Gilbert," Grandma said briskly. "We shall go to Argument House right now. We shall *fast-track* this application! We shall get clearance *immediately*."

Gilbert shook his head. "It is never immediate, Dorabel," he said, gloomily. "Clearance takes months."

Grandma snorted. "Months?" she said. "Preposterous!"

She pulled herself up to her full height. "Between us, Gilbert – *both* government advisers – we shall set the wheels in motion TODAY!"

Then she turned to Mervikk. "Mervikk," she said. "Clearance may take a short while. However, we *will* get it. Then we shall FIND the grimbleshank plant! We shall shake its petals, and gather its seeds!"

"I can wait, Flo's-gran," Mervikk said. "I can wait."

Then we heard cheeping from the hallway. Flibben – awake, alert and out of his cot. Cheeping. VERY loudly.

"Besides," said Mervikk, beaming, "I have training plans for Flibben!"

*

We trained Flibben to track all day. Tracking simple things at first. Food. Then his favourite toy. And then – me.

Mervikk crouched down next to him. "Flibben, son," Mervikk beamed, waving one of my socks from yesterday in Flibben's face. "Now – it's time to track Flo!"

He turned to me. "Hide, Flo," he said. "But hide well! We don't want Flibben to spot you – he needs to sniff you out."

"Oh, I can do that, Mervikk," I said – and I couldn't help grinning. "I can hide VERY well."

Then I got out a small silver case. Opened it up. And there it was – jiggling quietly on its velvet cushion.

My wand. My short stubby wand.

Grandma gave me the wand, and she's teaching me spells. So far I can do two different transforming spells. And this – the spell I was about to do. A thirty-minute invisibility spell.

"*Abrakkida Sagallik, Viderik Non Possi*," I said, in the special singsong voice, with all the wandwaving – just like Grandma taught me. "*Tridekkem, Minokkit, Nonune!*"

A shower of stardust shot out of the end of my wand. It swirled all around me – and I disappeared.

(The witches in charge of this book want me to point out that NO witchchild should use a wand. And that a witchchild who wishes to track down a fairy nest should simply discuss the WHOLE SITUATION with a responsible grown-up.)

Flibben got better and better at tracking me, slapping his flippers together when he sniffed me out.

Then, for his last bit of tracking that day, I chose a VERY tricky spot – the herb garden. Round at the front of the house, and full of strong spicy smells to confuse him.

I crouched on the ground, invisible. Tucked behind a big sprawling wispenniola.

Then – next door, a skyrider landed. The flexipod opened, and out stepped a witch. A witch in robes of shimmering silver…

Grimmelda Hurlstruk.

Straight away I heard the front door of Jasmonikka Villa open. And Tremblikkon Stoop came running out. "Madam," he said – and he was gulping. "The crew – they want more money. *Danger* money."

"Danger money…?" said that soft silky voice. "DANGER money?"

Now Tremblikkon Stoop was quaking. "Because of the *risk*," he said. "Because of last time…"

Grimmelda stared at Tremblikkon Stoop. "There IS no danger, Stoop," she said. "There IS no risk. And there will be no more money."

Tremblikkon Stoop gulped more. "And one more thing," he said. "The searider with the, err … *cargo*. It was followed. By a unicorn."

"A unicorn…" said Grimmelda, with a hiss in her voice, "or a *semblawitch*?"

"They shook him off," said Tremblikkon Stoop. "Created a fog. But all the same—"

"This semblawitch," hissed Grimmelda, "who *is*

he, Stoop? Who IS he?"

Then she strode into the house, Tremblikkon Stoop scurrying behind her.

✦

That night I lay awake. Questions, thoughts, worries – all going round and round in my head…

The Trigoggladron… If *only* I could have asked it about Dad.

My Shudders… What did they *see*?

And those conversations, those puzzling conversations. The one just now – about the danger money, the risk…

And the one earlier – all those fears of Tremblikkon Stoop, the report he mentioned…

What did it all *mean*?

Until – at last – I fell asleep. Fell into deep muddled dreams. Of fairies with huge orange antlers. Of big bulging Trigoggladron eyes. Of a soft silky voice and cold staring eyes. Of the witchman, the caped and masked witchman. And the huge white unicorn…

Then I woke, early next morning.

Opened *Wild and Wonderful Witchglobe*. Turned to page 364. And sat, staring. Staring at the pages in front of me – full of unicorns.

And a box – right there, on the right-hand page…

FACT OR FAKE?

Over one hundred years ago, Harken Omp made headlines in the Shiverlands after falling from the back of a unicorn. Harken was seven years old when he took his tumble. He landed, head-first, on the ground.

Harken was not harmed – but it seemed that, although Harken was not BORN a glottawitch, the fall had MADE him one. For from then on, Harken was able to speak every single language of the witchglobe!

Many witchmedics thought it was trickery. That Harken was a fake, a glottawitch all along. That it was a plan hatched by the Omp family – already known as tricksters and rogues.

But some witchmedics believed Harken. Said it was impossible for a small witchboy to hide a mega-magiskill like glottawitchery. That he was a medical marvel.

Witchmedics argue to this day about whether it was fact or fake. What they do know is this. There has been no other incident of a fall causing glottawitchery before or since – anywhere on the witchglobe!

I sat there, head spinning. That witchboy, Harken Omp – his fall, his bump to the head, caused glottawitchery. *Glottawitchery*...

A mega-magiskill – a skill witches are BORN with.

So Dad – his fall, into the Ice Volcano... Could the same thing have happened to Dad? Could Dad be the *second* witch ever to develop a mega-magiskill from a fall, from a bump to the head?

Not glottawitchery – but *semblawitchery*...

I thought back. To that mysterious masked witchman. How I felt when I saw him. How he stood, how he moved, how everything about him reminded me of Dad...

And inside me, the feeling grew stronger and stronger. That mysterious masked witchman – it *was* Dad. It WAS...

Then I heard footsteps, and my door flew open.

Mervikk was there – face palest green. "Flibben!" he said. "He's gone!"

Chapter 30

"Flibben!" shouted Mervikk, running into the back garden. "Flibben! Where are you?"

We checked all over, but there was no sign of him. So we ran to the front of the house. And there he was, in next door's garden, heading straight up the steps of the huge, high skysplitter.

We leapt over the fence, and ran towards the skysplitter. Just as Flibben shot inside.

"I'm fetching him!" said Mervikk. And he hurtled up the shiny silver staircase.

I looked left and right – but there was no one around. No one to ask. So I ran after Mervikk, and in through the open flexipod doors.

I stared. We were in a long corridor – with LOTS of doors off it. Open doors. Cabin doors.

But which one was Flibben in?

"I'm trying this one first," said Mervikk, running through the open door of the nearest cabin.

It was a sitting room. One big sofa, with a very high back, two big armchairs. And an open porthole. But no sign of Flibben.

"We'll search them all," I said. "We'll find him. He's safe somewhere. Don't worry."

But then the front door of Jasmonikka Villa burst open – and I heard feet, stomping nearer, then a voice. A big booming voice…

"My Witchen Day speech," the voice boomed. "Stoop, I must practise my speech!"

Me and Mervikk stared down from the porthole. Here he came, Mr Potions2Go, strutting into the front garden, Tremblikkon Stoop scurrying behind him.

We looked at each other. What should we do? Go out, and tell them we were looking for Flibben? Or stay here and keep quiet?

Now Mr Potions2Go blew one sharp blast on a whistle.

A boggle came bounding out of the house. A

guard boggle. Big and broad, with a shiny black coat.

"Seek!" ordered Mr Potions2Go, pointing. "Check! For INTRUDERS! For LURKERS! For SNOOPERS! For that PESKY WITCHMAN!"

I watched every step the boggle took. Watched it go sniffing all around the front garden, pacing along the fence, round all the edges. Then it turned back towards Mr Potions2Go. Lay down at his feet. And stared straight up at him.

I stared too. Stared and stared.

That boggle – something about it was making me tingle. Tingle from head to foot. Those eyes. So bright, so alert…

Now Mr Potions2Go was taking out a sheet of paper. "My speech, Stoop," he boomed, frowning. "You are *sure* there will be witchhacks there? Outside my Hurlstruk Happy Home?"

"There will, Sir," said Tremblikkon Stoop. "From *Haggnews*, and the *Haggspit Herald*."

"Good," said Mr Potions2Go. "Because I am NOT giving my speech, NOT handing out Witchen Day presents – bought with *my* money – to those orphans without LOTS of witchhacks, LOTS of publicity."

Now Mr Potions2Go cleared his throat and started reading from the sheet. "I am here today," he said, "*not* as a successful and powerful businesswitch – but as an ordinary witchman."

He stopped. Wiped his brow. "Ridiculous speech," he huffed. "Ordinary? I am NOT ordinary."

"A little humility always works well, Sir," said Tremblikkon Stoop.

Mr Potions2Go sighed. "If I *must*," he said, then carried on reading. "Seeing these faces before me," he said. "Faces of dear little witchchildren—"

He stopped. Scowled. "Yuk," he said. "I dislike ALL witchchildren. Grubby creatures – always asking silly questions. And orphans are the worst of the lot. *Ghastly* little things."

The boggle stretched. Yawned. Got to its feet.

"I consider this Hurlstruk Happy Home my greatest achievement," Mr Potions2Go read. "Greater than any business deal I have made."

He stopped. "Pah!" he said. "*Pah*, Stoop! The Hurlstruk Happy Home – it is a NUISANCE, not an achievement."

"It makes you look good, Sir," said Tremblikkon Stoop. "Caring. Like Aggratikka Thropistikkan."

Mr Potions2Go snorted. "Yuk and DOUBLE yuk!" he said. "Nincompoop! Doing good works because she actually WANTS to!"

He snorted again. "And that Skritchett witch –

she's a nincompoop too. Pulling out of our deal. Telling me off about the forest trolls. The CHEEK of it!"

Just then – a skychatter rang.

Tremblikkon Stoop answered it. "Yes…" he said. "Yes… No… Yes… At once…"

And I could see – just from his face, that Tremblikkon Stoop was panicking. Palest green, forehead glistening.

"Sir," he said. "Bad news. VERY bad news. The captain of the searider – he just called me. The crew… It seems … during the dumping of the, er, *cargo*, they were *attacked*."

Then he pulled a map out of his robe pocket. A big map.

I went cold.

That map – it was of the *Wild Isles*…

Now Tremblikkon Stoop was pointing. Straight at a Wild Isle with a big red circle drawn all around it.

"First attack was here," he said, pointing. "Near the landing spot. And the second, the third attacks – near the imms' dump. The crew were lucky to escape."

He mopped at his forehead with a big spotted handkerchief. "Attacked by VERY strange creatures indeed," he said faintly.

"Strange creatures?" boomed Mr Potions2Go. "What on earth do you mean, Stoop – STRANGE CREATURES?"

"It seems, Sir," he said, more faintly than ever, "we may have created an island of … well – MUTANTS!"

Mutants… MUTANTS…

My head was spinning.

Mr Potions2Go – he was dumping his old imms on one of the *Wild Isles*. And now – it was covered in MUTANTS.

But Mr Potions2Go just waved his hand about. "So, Stoop?" he said. "So what? A few little mutants. We'll just have to start using *another* Wild Isle."

I could NOT believe it. Nor could Tremblikkon Stoop. He stood there, quaking, his mouth right open.

"But, Sir," he said, nervously. "Suppose there are more mutants? Suppose some are SWIMMING mutants, FLYING mutants? Suppose the mutants *spread*? Spread to other islands? And to here? To the mainland? To Kronebay?"

"Oh, pish – the government can deal with a few mutants," said Mr Potions2Go, looking exasperated. "The government are used to dealing with outbreaks of ghastly creatures."

Then Mr Potions2Go stopped. Frowned. Bit his lip, and looked worried. Then his eyes started darting about. "Although..." he said – and now I could hear panic in his voice, "suppose we get found out? Then we are in *trouble*."

He snatched the map off Tremblikkon Stoop. "The map," he said, panicking more. "HIDE the map! No one must know about the map!"

But just then the boggle leapt across the front garden and stood by the far fence, barking and barking.

"An INTRUDER!" bellowed Mr Potions2Go. "Listening! SPYING! I knew it!"

He blew three sharp blasts on his whistle and witchmen came running from inside the house. "Seize him!" he shrieked pointing at the far fence. "The intruder! Seize him, wherever he is!"

The whole team went surging across the garden, surging towards the fence – just as the boggle came leaping BACK.

With one huge bound, it leapt at Mr Potions2Go. It grabbed the map in its teeth – then the boggle was gone.

Gone.

And up into the sky soared a witchman. A caped

and masked witchman, arms pointing upwards, map in his robe pocket.

Then he too was gone. In his place – a huge white unicorn. Soaring up and up through the sky, strong wings beating as it flew straight out to sea… Straight out towards the Wild Isles…

Towards the island of MUTANTS.

Part
Three

Chapter 31

I stared up at the sky. Tingles raced up and down my spine. I was filled – head to foot – with longing. Such SUCH longing. Longing so strong, so powerful, I could hardly breathe.

That witchman – that caped and masked witchman – there was no doubt in my mind. None at all.

It was Dad. It *was*.

My missing dad. He was here. *Here*. So close I could almost have reached out and touched him. But now – he was gone.

Heading straight out to the Wild Isles.

"THIEF! VILLAIN!" roared Mr Potions2Go, shaking his fist up at the sky. "Bring back my map! Bring it *baaaack*!"

Now Mr Potions2Go grabbed Tremblikkon Stoop by the arm. "Stoop," he said – wild panic in his eyes. "He must be *stopped*! That villain – he must be STOPPED!"

He clutched harder, his whole body trembling. "That villain must NOT find the island, Stoop!" he said. "He'll get pictures – *proof* of the illegally dumped imms!"

Then he gave a big gasp. "And the fines, Stoop!" he gasped. "They'll RUIN me! And my houses – I'll be forced to sell three, four, maybe even FIVE of my houses! And some of my islands! And my seariders!"

Now tears – big fat ones – started spurting out of his eyes. "No more homes around the witchglobe!" he bawled. "No more holidays! No more cruises! And worse – I may be *disgraced*! I may have to return my Hovelhagg medal. My lovely shiny medal! I may even end up in PRISON! Among CRIMINALS AND THIEVES!"

Then – a voice spoke. "Daddy," the voice said. "All is *not* lost."

Grimmelda Hurlstruk. Dressed in robes of shimmering green. Darkest green – the deep green

236

of poison. Walking towards Mr Potions2Go.

"Stoop," she said, grey eyes staring. "I hear we have a problem."

Tremblikkon Stoop stood, quivering. "Mutants," he whispered. "MUTANTS. Caused by *us*."

"Mutants," Grimmelda said quietly. "How … *unfortunate*."

Mr Potions2Go scrabbled at her arm. "Grimmelda," he said. "*Help* Daddy! Daddy doesn't want to sell his lovely homes. Daddy wants to KEEP them! Daddy doesn't want to go to prison. Not nasty stinky prison with ORDINARY witches! It is so UNFAIR! Me – ME! A witchman who builds homes for *orphans*!"

Grimmelda put a finger to her lips. "Daddy, hush," she said. "Do I not *always* solve your problems? When you were caught handing out bribes to win government contracts… Caught banking your money in colonies you shouldn't… Did I not *fix* those problems for you?"

"You did, Grimmelda, you *did*," nodded Mr Potions2Go. "So fix this! FIX THIS!"

"Oh, I shall, Daddy," Grimmelda said. "Have no fear."

She paused. Stared up at the sky. "That masked witchman," she said, "we shall … deal with him."

"But how? *How?*" said Mr Potions2Go. "How

will we deal with him? How can we FIND him? The sky is very BIG, Grimmelda!"

Grimmelda held up one hand, long bony fingers glinting with jewels. "We cannot find him, Daddy," she said.

Then she smiled a thin, tight smile. "Which is why, Daddy, we let *him* find the ISLAND."

Then she turned. "Stoop," she said. "Summon the crew. We leave for the Wild Isle RIGHT NOW."

✦

I crouched, trembling. Stared at Mervikk. He stared back. Both of us too shocked to speak.

Then we heard feet. Running from the house and the grounds of Jasmonikka Villa. Feet, thudding towards the skysplitter.

We hid. Hid in the only place we could think of. Hurled ourselves behind the big high-backed sofa.

Feet thudded up the steps, and along the corridor. Voices shouted orders. Doors, portholes – they all hissed shut. Then – with one huge roar from the enormous engine – the skysplitter soared away from the ground.

The force of that take-off took my breath away. The surge of power from that engine, the sense of great speed, was like NOTHING I had felt before. Me and Mervikk were flung against the cabin wall as the skysplitter powered up through the sky, then levelled.

We picked ourselves up – then froze. We could hear footsteps. Two pairs of feet, heading along the corridor. Towards THIS cabin…

And in they came.

We cowered behind the sofa, as a voice boomed out from one of the armchairs. A voice we knew VERY well.

"Grimmelda, Daddy is BAFFLED!" the voice boomed. "Why do we let that masked witchman find the island? *Why?* He will get proof of the imms. He will RUIN me!"

And now – that soft silky voice, a voice that chilled me right through. "He will not, Daddy…" said the voice. "Not if we are there *first*. And we have the skysplitter. Ten – *fifteen* – times faster than a unicorn."

"Grimmelda," Mr Potions2Go boomed. "Daddy is STILL baffled."

"Hush, Daddy," said Grimmelda. "I have a call to make. Then I shall explain."

It was a very short call. One word only. "Disconnect," she said softly.

And then – "The Shimmering," she said. "It is now switched off."

The Shimmering… Switched off…

I thought of Mum. Of what she said the day the Hurlstruks arrived…

"Contacts… All businesswitches must build contacts! Contacts in important places. Contacts who can pull strings. Get things done."

So Grimmelda Hurlstruk – she had contacts. Contacts who could turn off the Shimmering. And THAT was how the searider got through. The searider, full of old imms to be dumped illegally.

And now – the skysplitter…

And us.

"This, Daddy, is the plan," said Grimmelda's soft voice. "We shall let our masked witchman find the island. And when he does – we will be waiting. This time, it is *our* turn to ambush HIM."

"An AMBUSH!" said Mr Potions2Go, with a gasp of excitement. "Yes, Grimmelda, I am LIKING the sound of an ambush!"

He paused. "And then what?" he demanded. "What happens *after* the ambush?"

"That masked protester – he is a semblawitch…" said that soft silky voice. "But he is also a *witchman*."

Then the voice paused. "And a witchman can be Erased," it said.

Erased… *Erased…*

240

No.

NO. Something inside me went cold. Icy cold.

Grimmelda Hurlstruk – even Grimmelda Hurlstruk – could *not* be planning an ERASING spell. A spell from the *Forbidden* list? The worst witch-harming magic of all? One of the three deadly spells no witch should EVER do?

Even Mr Potions2Go sounded shocked. "Grimmelda, is that a *good* plan?" he said. "Daddy is not entirely SURE it is a good plan."

"Daddy," said the voice. "Do you WANT to go to prison?"

"No, Grimmelda, no," he said. "There might be giant NIBBETS. Or bitey serpents. As well as thieves and criminals."

"So Daddy," the voice said, "we Erase him. Erase him until he is helpless. No memory. No understanding. *Nothing*. Helpless as the tiniest newborn witchbaby."

She paused.

"And then, Daddy," she said, "we leave him there. Erased and helpless. Alone on the island – at the mercy of MUTANTS!"

Chapter 32

I crouched there, shaking with anger, with FURY. An *Erasing* spell – there was no way back from an Erasing spell.

No. Grimmelda Hurlstruk could NOT do that. Not to Dad. Erase everything in his brain. Then abandon him.

No. *No*. NO.

I had just found Dad – I was NOT going to lose him. Not now.

I had to *stop* her. And I would.

But *how*? HOW?

There were four – maybe five – witchmen out

there. *And* Grimmelda. How could I POSSIBLY stop her?

Then I realised.

I *couldn't* stop Grimmelda. Not Grimmelda.

So I had to stop *Dad*. Somehow — I had to stop DAD…

Then the skysplitter screeched to a halt. It hovered, and landed.

We were here. On the island.

I could hear Mr Potions2Go leap to his feet. "Goody!" he boomed. "GOODY! Time to be ambushers!"

"No, Daddy," said the voice — harder now. "*I* will do the ambushing. Myself and the crew. Not you."

"Grimmelda, that is just not *fair*," Mr Potions2Go moaned. "Daddy doesn't WANT to stay behind."

"You are noisy and unreliable," said the voice. "And no good at hiding. You will give us away."

"But Daddy wants to HELP with the ambush," wailed Mr Potions2Go. "Daddy has never BEEN an ambusher before!"

"DO AS YOU ARE TOLD," said the voice — hard as steel now.

I could hear Mr Potions2Go scuffing his foot. "Okaaaaay," he said, sounding glum. "But promise to tell me ALL about the ambushing. PROMISE!"

"I promise," said the voice.

Then a bell rang – and feet came running to the doorway. "Stoop," said the voice. "Stay here. Attend to my father."

And – with a swish of her robes Grimmelda Hurlstruk was gone. Issuing orders, summoning the crew. Then I heard footsteps – feet running – the hiss of doors opening, a staircase lowering, more footsteps, then silence…

For a moment.

Until – "Stoop!" boomed Mr Potions2Go. "I want a MUTANT. I want a mutant as a pet. I have *never* had a pet mutant. I want one NOW."

"Sir," said Tremblikkon Stoop, sounding utterly shocked. "I can't *possibly* allow it."

"Can't allow it?" bellowed Mr Potions2Go. "CAN'T ALLOW IT? Very well, Stoop – I shall go ALONE!"

Then – "*Abrakkida Rune!*" his voice boomed out, and I heard the sounds of a body – Stoop's body – crumpling to the floor. And snoring, loud snoring. As the stomping feet of Mr Potions2Go headed out of the cabin, and towards the steps of the skysplitter.

✦

Me and Mervikk crawled out from behind the sofa, and stepped over the snoring Stoop.

Mervikk looked at me, shocked. "An *Erasing* spell!" he said, his face palest green. "Grimmelda... She's *evil*."

"Mervikk," I said, grabbing his arm. "That witchman, that semblawitch – he's my *dad*!"

Mervikk's mouth dropped right open. "Your dad?" he said. "But..."

"Trust me – he *is*. And I have to WARN him!" I said.

Then I ran. Ran for the skysplitter steps and stared around. At the beach. Paths winding away through tangles of trees. And cliffs. Towering cliffs, stretching up out of the sea.

The cliffs...

There – up there, that tallest cliff of all. Facing straight towards the mainland. Straight towards Kronebay. THAT was the place to warn Dad.

I ran, as fast as I could. Across the beach. Towards a path that twisted and turned, higher and higher.

I climbed and climbed, up towards that towering cliff.

I could hear Mervikk behind me, gasping his way up the path. Not me. I felt like I had wings on my feet.

Dad. I HAD to warn Dad. I *had* to get there.

I put everything else out of my head. And I ran.

Beating my way up the path, through tangled plants and twisted trees. And out of the trees, running along the cliff edge, waves crashing, far *far* below me. The wind buffeting and billowing around me as I ran.

Then I reached it – the very top of the cliff. And I stood and I stared, into the sky. Searching and searching…

And there it was.

A tiny white speck in the distance. Growing bigger and bigger, nearer and nearer.

Fingers fumbling, I unhooked the lantern from my belt. The tiny lantern – glinting green and gold – in my hand.

The lantern of the Valliants.

I waved my hands, and the lantern grew bigger. The flame grew brighter.

Bigger still, brighter still.

A beaming light of dazzling flame. Bright, strong light, soaring across the sky. Light shining as bright as the suns themselves.

Yes, Dad would see that.

Dad…

But maybe OTHER witches too. Other witches, somewhere, here on this island…

Or mutants. Attracted by the light…

No. NO. I would *not* think about that. I would NOT.

And now Mervikk was here, gasping beside me, as I waved my hand and began to spell out letters. One after another after another.

The secret code of the Valliants. Spelling out a warning – again and again and again…

DANGER
AMBUSH
DANGER
AMBUSH
DANGER
AMBUSH

"Dad," I whispered. "Remember. *Remember!*"

But *would* he? WOULD Dad remember? I just didn't know.

He remembered our tune, taught it to the snow trolls. But this… Would he remember *this*?

Dad *had* to remember. He HAD to.

But still – those huge beating wings grew nearer. Nearer and nearer and NEARER.

Shivers of fear ran right through me. Shivers of terror. He *didn't* remember. He just didn't remember.

But then – the unicorn stopped. It hovered…
And TURNED.

It turned and flew *away* from the island.

Just as, behind me, a voice boomed out. "You! Small witchgirl with the lantern. What are you DOING?"

Chapter 33

I turned. Mr Potions2Go was stomping towards me, bright green in the face, teeth gnashing.

"You were SIGNALLING!" he bellowed, staring up at the sky, at the tiny white speck in the distance.

Then he stamped his foot and shook his fist, right in my face. "You were *warning* that witchman – somehow you were WARNING him!" he bellowed. "You are a very BAD witchgirl!"

Now – at that moment I had two feelings surging through me.

First, relief. Total relief. The lantern – it had worked. Dad was safe. *Safe*.

But another feeling too…

FURY.

Fury at that pompous strutting witchman, standing there, bellowing at me, shaking his fist. Plotting to *Erase* my dad. And if he could bellow – then I could *yell*.

So I did. I yelled right in his face. "Yes, I *did* warn him," I yelled. "And it's not ME who's bad. It's you!"

Then I shrank the lantern, hooked it back on to my belt, and glared at him.

Mr Potions2Go looked astonished. And now he peered at me, eyes narrowed. "I know you," he said. "That Skritchett witch… Aren't you … yes, you ARE… You're her daughter!"

Then he turned to Mervikk, and jabbed a finger right at him. "And you, scruffy witchboy…" he said. "I've seen you before too."

Mervikk did NOT like a finger being jabbed at him. He glared up at Mr Potions2Go. "We heard you," he said. "On the skysplitter. You're practically a GANGSTER. Dumping all your old imms on this island!"

Mr Potions2Go's eyebrows shot up. He gasped. "STOWAWAYS!" he bellowed. "EAVES-DROPPERS! SIGNALLERS! Is there no END to your WICKEDNESS?"

Enough. I was *way* too cross to be scared. Mr Potions2Go – he was an IDIOT.

"Wickedness?" I said. "What about YOUR wickedness? The creatures on this island – you're *poisoning* them. Just so you can save money!"

"And you're GREEDY," said Mervikk. "You're already rich. You don't need *more* money."

Mr Potions2Go gaped at him. "Of course I do," he said, eyes popping. "A witchman can NEVER have too much money."

"And what about the Erasing spell?" I said. "You were planning an ERASING spell on that witchman!"

Mr Potions2Go looked down at his feet. Scuffed his shoes. "It wasn't MY idea," he said, a bit sulkily. "I NEVER liked that Erasing spell idea. In fact—"

He stopped.

Two little bobbentuft babies were hopping along the path. Small, fluffy, and chattering to each other.

A gooey sort of look spread across the face of Mr Potions2Go. "Ah," he said, head tilted to one side. "Baby *bobbentufts*!"

He crouched down. Pulled two Yumyums out of his robe pocket. Held them out in his palm. "Here, little fellows," he said. "Here."

The two baby bobbentufts hopped towards him. Then one grabbed both Yumyums.

The other bobbentuft was NOT happy. It grabbed them both back.

Mr Potions2Go wagged his finger. "Now, now," he said. "Share nicely."

But the bobbentufts didn't.

Backwards and forwards they grabbed. Both getting crosser and crosser and crosser…

And then – the eyes of one baby bobbentuft started to *glow*.

Mr Potions2Go stared, eyes popping. "What's happening?" he gasped. "What's happening to the baby?"

Now it was growing bigger. Five, six, seven – TWENTY – times the size of the other. Two twisty tusks were sprouting out of its head. Its chattering mouth filled up with fangs.

The other baby bobbentuft squeaked with terror. Then hopped away, as fast as it could.

Not fast enough…

The creature – the HUGE mutant creature – pounced. Grabbed the baby bobbentuft – and, with one leap, disappeared behind a vast pile of boulders.

It was *horrible*.

I blocked my ears. But I could still hear – the tiny

squeaking sounds, the huge snarling sounds. And then…

The crunching, grinding, chewing sounds.

Mr Potions2Go stood there. Stock-still. Mouth open. Listening.

Finally – there was silence…

But not for long.

Because Mr Potions2Go started to howl. "The *baby*…" he howled, tears streaming down his face. "It's gone! I am SO sorry, baby! So *so* SORRY!"

Then I heard a voice behind us. "Daddy," the voice said. "Be quiet."

I turned.

There she was. Grimmelda Hurlstruk, with Tremblikkon Stoop and the crew.

"Grimmelda," Mr Potions2Go howled. "We have done a terrible *terrible* thing. The baby – it's GONE!"

Then he blew his nose. Loudly.

Grimmelda just stared. "Daddy," she said. "It is time to go. To leave this island."

Then she paused. Turned her gaze on me, on Mervikk. "Time to leave these *witchchildren*," she said. And the look in her eyes – it made me go cold.

Mr Potions2Go gasped. He staggered backwards. "Leave the witchchildren?" he said, eyes popping. "But… But … Grimmelda – remember there are *mutants*. I saw one! They might get guzzled by a MUTANT."

"We can hope so, Daddy," said Grimmelda.

Mr Potions2Go was shaking his head. "No, Grimmelda," he said. "No, no. NO. It's wrong. I *know* it's wrong. And the Erasing spell – that was wrong. Grimmelda, we must RETHINK."

Then – from somewhere deep in the island, came howls. Loud howls.

"Sir, Madam," said Tremblikkon Stoop, getting out a big handkerchief and mopping his forehead. "We must *leave*. Remember – the creatures. We have been lucky so far – but our luck will NOT hold out."

Mr Potions2Go started shaking his head. "Grimmelda, we canNOT leave the witchchildren," he said. "But I know – I know what to do!"

He crouched down next to me, and grabbed my arm. "Now, see here, missy. I promise not to dump ANY MORE imms on this island – but YOU have to promise not to tell – and in return I shall buy you both GIFTS. Lovely gifts."

I gaped. So did Mervikk.

"So," he said eagerly. "Name your gift. What is it you want, missy? I heard you playing the firkelhorn out in your garden. Would you like a new one? A lovely pink shiny firkelhorn?"

Then he turned to Mervikk. "And you? What would you like? A gritterback herd? Or an island? I could buy EACH of you an island – two are up for sale this very minute off the coast of Fangway. Name your gift."

"Daddy," said Grimmelda. "Stop wasting time. These witchchildren canNOT be bought. And now we must go."

Mr Potions2Go stood up. Folded his arms. Stuck his bottom lip out. "Grimmelda – I am OVERRULING you. We canNOT leave the witchchildren here. It's wrong, and—"

"*Abrakkida Rune*," said Grimmelda softly, pointing her spellstick.

Mr Potions2Go stopped in mid-sentence. His eyeballs went spinning, round and round and round. Then he fell to the ground.

Grimmelda put her spellstick away, and turned to the crew – the five burly witchmen.

"Carry my father to the skysplitter," she said. "When he wakes, he will remember nothing of this trip."

Then she paused. Stared at the crew, unblinking. "And know this," she said softly. "Should any details of this trip become known – there will be

CONSEQUENCES."

The crew – those five burly witchmen – they were *terrified*.

Then she turned. Stared at me, stared at Mervikk. As if she could see right inside our heads.

And I shivered.

"So, Florence Skritchett…" she said, sounding thoughtful. "*Why* is it you were so concerned about warning that witchman, I wonder?"

She looked up at the sky, the empty sky. Then back at me. "Your efforts are in vain," she said. "For I shall FIND him in the end. And when I do…"

She tailed away. Shook her head sadly. Then tilted it to one side.

"Poor little witchchildren," she said. "Now, we must say our farewells. And leave you – *alone* on this island."

And once again, from deep in the island – came howls. Louder howls. "Or perhaps not ALL alone," she said, with a small smile.

Her smile grew wider. "I wish you all the luck in the world…" she said. "I do believe you will need it."

Then Grimmelda Hurlstruk turned – and walked away.

Chapter 34

Alone. Me and Mervikk were alone on a cliff top. Stuck on one of the Wild Isles.

I stared around me.

The skysplitter was gone. Dad was gone...

Everyone was gone.

And the island – it was so big, so scary, stretching away all around us. Towering cliffs of jagged grey rocks. Tangles of trees – all bent and twisted, battered by the wild winter winds from the Shiverlands.

All the sounds. So many sounds.

Rustling sounds. Screeching sounds. And howls – the loud howls of something.

Something… But what?

Beside me, Mervikk stood, teeth chattering. "What do we do, Flo?" he said. "What do we DO? No one knows we're here. And there's no skychatter signal – no way of letting anyone know."

He looked around, panicking. Totally panicking. "Can we build a raft?" he said. "Get ourselves off the island? Or can we signal? Make a big HELP sign out of leaves? What? WHAT?"

A roar filled the air, and Mervikk grabbed my arm. "I'm scared, Flo," he said. "How long will we last here, with MUTANTS? A few hours? A few days? A week?"

His head spun around. "And where are they – the mutants? They could be *anywhere*. Suppose there's a mutant over there, behind the trees? Or in those bushes? Or behind that big rock?"

Now Mervikk was quaking. "And how will we *know* which the mutants are, Flo? How can we tell? Because if that little bobbentuft turned out to be mutant – then *any* creature here can be mutant. ANY CREATURE AT ALL!"

Then – we heard rustling. And something small and blue shot straight up the path towards Mervikk.

"Flibben!" gasped Mervikk, scooping him up. "You found us!"

Flibben cheeped. And Mervikk fed him some little seeds and berries – woddelflomp mix – from his pocket.

Something squawked nearby.

Mervikk's head shot up. He looked all around. "What was that?" he said. "*Another* mutant? ANOTHER? If that's another – that's two mutants in one hour. And if there's two mutants every *hour*, then that's FORTY-EIGHT mutants in JUST ONE DAY!"

Flibben cheeped again.

"And suppose there's one *worse*?" Mervikk whispered, feeding Flibben more mix. "One much MUCH worse?"

The squawking grew louder. Mervikk held Flibben closer. "And Flibben," Mervikk said, "my son… If anything happens to him, I'll *never* forgive myself. Flibben, he—"

I HAD to do it.

I put my hand right over Mervikk's mouth. "Mervikk, STOP," I said. "Stop talking. And start *thinking*. We need food, shelter and water. All three. Before it's dark."

I was trying VERY hard to keep my voice calm – and not wobbly like Mervikk's voice was. But I didn't feel calm. Not one bit.

Because the suns were sinking now. The sky was turning darker. Night was on the way. And I did NOT want to think about the night.

But – no matter how hard I tried to stop them – other thoughts were spilling into my head.

Thoughts of the fairy, the bobbentuft – how those tiny little creatures grew and grew and GREW… And thoughts of my Shudders. Those things, those glimpses – what did I see?

"Food, shelter, water, then…" Mervikk said, nodding and trying to sound calm. "But which way do we go?"

I stared around. We had to choose a path, but which one? There were so many. Small winding paths – made by paws, by claws, by hooves. By creatures of the island – but what kind of creatures?

Ordinary creatures? Or something else? Something not ordinary *at all*.

"That one," I said, pointing. "And tread VERY carefully. Do NOT make anything angry."

Mervikk nodded again. "Not mutant hunting," he said, trembling. "Mutant AVOIDING."

"Remember Mr Prankett…" I said. "When the glompjaw escaped from the zoo? What he told us?"

Mervikk nodded.

Because Mr Prankett wrote a whole lot of tips on the greenboard. About avoiding a glompjaw attack…

DO NOT RUN! THAT WILL TRIGGER THE HUNTING INSTINCT OF THE GLOMPJAW!

DO NOT LOOK THE GLOMPJAW IN THE EYE! IT WILL FEEL THREATENED!

DO BACK AWAY SLOWLY FROM THE GLOMPJAW!

DO MAKE YOURSELF LOOK BIGGER! IF THE GLOMPJAW APPROACHES – SHOUT AND STRETCH OUT YOUR ARMS!

"Those tips – they could work with mutants," I said.

Mervikk nodded. "Bound to," he said, teeth clacking more. "Mutants are most probably almost IDENTICAL to glompjaws."

Then we both gulped.

"Another thing," I said, trying to sound confident. "If – just suppose – we *do* make anything angry, there are TWO of us. So we have the advantage."

Mervikk nodded. "We utterly DO have the

advantage," he said, teeth clacking more and more. "We're a team, Flo."

At his feet, Flibben cheeped, as Mervikk clicked the lead to his collar. "A team of three," Mervikk said.

And we all started walking. Looking left, looking right. Listening to sounds. Sounds of things rustling in the shadows of the trees.

I jumped.

Something brushed against my leg. A nibbet. A small, bright blue nibbet. Then more. One, two, three, four, five nibbets – scampering across the path.

And, through the trees – whiskers. Long twitching whiskers.

Whiskers of what? *What?*

Then they were gone.

Something was snuffling. Snuffling down one of those dark paths. Down in the trees. Snuffling nearer and nearer.

I froze. So did Mervikk. As, snuffling out from the undergrowth – came a windsniffer. A small bristling windsniffer. Snuffling along, looking for grubbles.

It saw us. Stopped. Stared. And moved on.

Then Mervikk grabbed my arm. "Flo! *Flo!*" he said. "Look! Up there! The grimbleshank plant!"

I stared. Was he right? There, twined around the

lowest branch of the tree – was that the grimbleshank plant? The cure for Stumbles?

Mervikk was already scrambling up the trunk of the tree. Hauling himself along the branch. He plucked the flower. "Got it!" he said. But then, from up above him something *yawned*.

A splorg. A huge blubbery splorg. Dangling upside down, up high in the tree. Its big toothy mouth wide open in a yawn.

It opened its one big eye. It stared. Its mouth started to snarl…

A splorg does NOT like to be woken from sleep.

Mervikk scrambled down the tree – FAST. We ran along the path. Dived into the bushes and hid.

Then we waited. Quaking.

Nothing. No sounds of an angry splorg mutating. Just yawning noises. Then snores. The splorg was asleep once more.

Mervikk stared down at the flower in his hand. He shook his head. "Wrong sort of leaves," he said sadly.

But I had spotted something. Food. "Mervikk," I said, pointing. "Blorberries! A big patch of them!"

Me and Mervikk stuffed blorberries into our mouths, as fast as we could. Flibben too – snuffling and guzzling, blue blorberry juice dribbling down the sides of his beak.

Then I remembered something Mum said to me and Mervikk on Kraggen, when we found a patch of blorberries to pick...

"Where you find blorberries – you will always find speedelbrott."

We did. A big clump of speedelbrott. Enough to fill our stomachs now – and our pockets for later.

Better still, a few hundred metres down the path, I saw something else.

A gap in the rocks. A gap the size of a witchkid...

And inside the gap – a big CAVE.

Chapter 35

We huddled against one wall. We had shelter — but the cave felt dark and scary. Full of shadowy corners, all lit by the flickering flame of the lantern.

But no creatures seemed to live here. No serpents hissing on the floor. No bats hanging from the roof...

Then — something shot across the cave floor. A small hairy something with lots of legs.

A *scuttlepin*.

I trembled. I always do when I see scuttlepins.

Mervikk clutched my arm. "Suppose that's a MUTANT," he whispered, quaking. "Look, it's staring at us. Maybe it's ANNOYED we're in its cave. And its eyes – are they *glowing*?"

"Mervikk, calm down," I said, trying not to tremble. "Its eyes are NOT glowing, they're just shining because of the lantern."

Then the scuttlepin shot back across the cave floor. But this time, Flibben shot after it, beak snapping up and down. Trying to catch it.

Mervikk leapt up and grabbed him. "Flibben, *no*!" he said, panicking, as the scuttlepin raced up the cave wall. "NO! STOP! Don't make it *angry*!"

Flibben looked shocked.

Mervikk had NEVER told him off before.

He stared. Cheeped. Slapped his front flippers together. And I could see – Flibben did NOT know how to feel about being told off. Upset … or angry.

Then Flibben hung his head. Sniffed. Cheeped sadly. Slunk off into a corner, curled up and turned his back on us.

Just then – I heard a noise. A faint noise. Low and rumbling.

A shiver went right through me.

There were lots of noises on this island – strange, eerie noises. But this one… What was it?

Mervikk heard it too. "Is that thunder?" he said. "Or something growling? Some creature?"

"I don't think so," I said. "I don't think it's either."

"What then?" said Mervikk. "What *is* it?"

"I think…" I said. "I think it's coming from under the *ground*."

We stared at each other. And – or was I imagining it? – under my feet, did the cave floor *quiver*?

"I don't like it," said Mervikk. "I want that noise – whatever it is – to *stop*. NOW."

The noise did.

Then Mervikk swallowed. "I'm *thirsty*," he said. "SO thirsty…"

I did NOT want to leave the cave. Not after that low rumbling sound we just heard…

What was it? *Where* was it?

But we had to find water – and soon. Before the shadows lengthened and the sky grew dark. Before the night was here.

So we left the cave. Walked down the path on trembling legs – then we heard it, not far away. The splashing sounds of a fast-flowing river…

And there it was. Ahead of us, through the trees. A little clearing, and a river. Small waterfalls, splashing and gushing and dropping their way down the mountainside.

Scrubby bushes and rocks hugged the bank.

A huge weeper tree leaned over the river, leaves trailing down into the water.

Then – we heard chirrupping. And here they came.

A flock of chirruppellas. Hopping all around us, black eyes staring.

Mervikk lifted up Flibben, and went treading – slowly, carefully – through the chirruppellas. He crouched down by the river, put Flibben down, and started scooping up water.

And THAT was when I saw them...

Footprints.

Here, in the soft ground of the clearing.

Huge footprints.

Some four-footed creature. Four webbed feet and four clawed toes.

Some *enormous* creature...

I looked around. The bushes, the rocks – they were all scorched.

Scorched.

Shivers went through me.

Those sounds – the sounds of water, splashing water... And the shapes, the bushes, the rocks, the weeper tree...

They were sounds, shapes – shadowy shapes – from my Shudders.

I started to tremble.

"Mervikk," I said. "Mervikk…" But my words came out as a croak.

Mervikk was standing up now, water dripping from his chin. Staring up at the weeper tree. "The grimbleshank plant!" he gasped, pointing. "It's up there. It's THERE!"

I looked up. Saw flowers, climbing their way round the end of one outstretched branch. And Mervikk, scrambling up the branches of the weeper tree.

Then he was there, on the end of the branch. Lunging forward, as far as he could. But, just as he reached out to grab at the grimbleshank plant – he lost his grip and went tumbling down.

"Mervikk!" I screamed, as he landed – with a big thud, on the riverbank. Right by a rock.

And THAT was when a small chirruppella leapt out from the rocks. Angry and threatened. Hissing and baring its tiny sharp teeth.

I knew straightaway. That chirruppella – it had a *nest*. Right there, right in the rocks…

Then – its eyes began to GLOW.

Part
Four

Chapter 36

It took *seconds*. SECONDS for that tiny chirruppella to grow, to change – into something *huge*. So huge, so terrifying it froze me to the spot.

Like some kind of dragon – a wild dragon of old. But worse. Much worse.

The creature crouched, hissing and snarling and spitting. Crouched – on four scaly legs, on four webbed feet with long spiky claws. Claws raking at the ground.

And the *size* of it. Even crouched, it was four, five – *six* – times my height. With scales all over, like glinting green armour. With strong spiny wings, and a long spiky tail.

And those eyes – those g l o w i n g green eyes. Eyes glowing with rage, with fury.

Then it opened its long toothy snout. And it SNARLED.

It snarled down at Mervikk – standing, mouth open, hair on end. Not able to move, not one single step…

But he *had* to. He HAD to. And so did I.

"Run, Mervikk! RUN!" I screamed, leaping towards him.

Too late.

The creature *pounced*. It snatched Mervikk up. Lifted him high, clutched him tight in its huge curving claws.

Mervikk screamed. He wriggled, he kicked, he battered at the creature. "Let me GO!" he screamed. "Put me DOWN!"

But the creature held Mervikk still closer. Close to its huge knobbly head. Close to its huge snarling snout. Then – those huge spiny wings began to unfurl and to *flap*.

No, NO.

It was going to take off! To fly away with Mervikk!

So I did the only thing I could think of. I ran at its long spiky tail. Grabbed at it – and *clung on*.

The creature snarled. It turned, snout snapping. Its tail whipped left, then right. Trying and trying to shake me off.

But still I clung on. I was *not* letting go. I was NOT.

Then, with a roar of rage, it tried to take off. With one, two, *three* strong flaps of its wings, it tried.

But it *couldn't*. Not with me clinging on to that long swishing tail. Destroying its balance.

"Put him *down*!" I shrieked. "Put him DOWN!"

And then … the creature *did* put him down.

It opened those huge curving claws, and dropped him.

Mervikk tumbled to the ground. Landed, with a thud, and lay there, stunned. And still I clung on as the creature's tail whipped from side to side.

But then – all of a sudden – it *stopped*.

I lost my grip. Went flying, tumbling, through the air. Then I landed…

Right beside Mervikk.

We lay there, both of us, too dazed to move.

And above us, the towering creature hunched. Eyes glowing, snout snarling.

Then it swiped. Swiped at Mervikk with one huge claw. Swiped at me. Missed us deliberately.

Then it hissed … and it *waited*.

I dragged Mervikk to his feet. "Run!" I gasped. "RUN! It's waiting. It wants to chase us – to *hunt*!"

I knew then. That creature, that dragon, that mutant – it was hunting in the ways of the wild dragons of old. The ways of chirruppellas today.

✳

We DID run. Running was all my panicking brain could think of to do.

That creature – there was no way to fight it.

We had to run. Run – and *hide*. Hide FAST. Somewhere that creature couldn't get us...

Like the cave.

Me, Mervikk – we went running through the trees. Running as fast as we could. Tripping and stumbling. Terrified.

Knowing that huge creature was right behind us. That those snarls, those swipes – they were part of the chase, part of the hunt.

That – with one pounce, one grab – the creature could reach us. Grab Mervikk, grab me, in those huge clawed feet.

So we ran.

We ran up the path. Ran, gasping for breath. Ran for the narrow gap in the rocks. Hurled ourselves through. Then cowered in the cave. Trembling.

Outside, the creature pounded around the

entrance. Pounded so hard the cave shook. Searching and sniffing for a way to get in.

"Are we safe in here?" said Mervikk, clutching on to me. "Are we *safe*?"

Then he shrieked.

Staring in through the gap in the rocks were those huge glowing eyes. And two huge nostrils – big black holes, flaring in fury.

Snarling noises bounced off the cave walls around us. Then – a huge roar. A roar so loud it made the cave tremble. The roar of a FURIOUS creature.

We cowered back against the cave wall.

"It can't get in," I said. "It *can't*. It's MUCH too big."

But then, from that huge snout – from those two flaring nostrils – came flames.

Thick flames of fire, swirling into the cave. Scorching the walls. Filling the air with thick heavy smoke.

Flames… Smoke…

And I knew. That creature, it couldn't get in – but it could force us OUT…

Smoke filled my eyes, my lungs. And me, Mervikk – we began to choke. Gasping and coughing, we ran to the gap. Then wriggled our way out. We *had* to. Even with that huge snarling creature waiting to pounce…

Except – it was gone.

✳

I went cold. ICY cold. "It's teasing us," I whispered, clutching Mervikk's arm. "Making us think we're safe. That's what chirruppellas do."

I've seen it happen in the garden at Kronebay. Chirruppellas, hunting nibbets. Teasing, playing – then disappearing. Letting the nibbet think it has got away…

Then POUNCING.

"Where is it?" Mervikk said, his voice trembling. "Where's it *gone*?"

We looked around.

Where was it hiding? Where? How could something SO big hide itself? There was nowhere for it to hide. Not here.

Then we heard a sound. A whimpering sound – high-pitched and piercing and loud. The sound of a panicking woddelflomp chick.

"*Flibben!*" said Mervikk, and he went running back down the path. Back towards the river.

I ran too.

Flibben was stuck. Tangled and struggling, caught by his trailing lead in a big patch of brambles. Trapped.

"Flibben!" Mervikk shrieked, hurling himself forwards. Then he crouched by the brambles. Started untangling Flibben. Setting him free.

He picked Flibben up. Stood, cradling him in his arms, as Flibben whimpered.

And THAT was when the creature pounced.

Soared down from the highest branches of a huge latchenboll tree. Then landed.

It roared. Took one step towards Mervikk. One step – then another. Then another...

Mervikk cowered away. Trembling, clutching Flibben. With nowhere to run. Behind them – the river. Ahead – the huge creature. And now, it was crouched. Ready to spring.

No. NO. I *had* to do something.

I fumbled in my robe pocket. Brought out my wand – my short stubby wand. Clutched it tight in trembling hands, then pointed it at Mervikk.

"*Abrakkida Sagallik, Viderik Non Possi*," I said, the words tumbling from my mouth. "*Tridekkem, Minokkit, Nonune.*"

A shower of stardust burst out of my wand, swirled all around Mervikk, all around Flibben...

And they were gone.

Invisible.

The creature looked left, looked right – it looked

all around. Then it threw back its huge knobbly head, and it ROARED. With confusion. With rage. With *fury*.

Then it turned. And it leapt…

Straight towards *me*.

Chapter 37

The TERROR I felt – I will *never* forget it…

With one huge bound, the creature leapt. Picked me up in its huge webbed feet. Clutched me tight in its strong curving claws. Shook me so hard it felt like every bone in my body was rattling…

Then, with one flap of those huge spiny wings, it soared up into the sky. Soared, with me dangling and struggling. Clutched in those claws – each bony claw big as my arm…

I will never EVER forget it. The touch of that cold scaly skin against mine. The sound of the snarls, and the hisses. The smell – strong and spicy – from that huge scaly body...

And the sight of the ground rushing by – far below, so SO far below...

✦

Questions – terrified questions – swirled round in my head.

Where was it taking me? Where would it land? Here, on this island? Or far FAR away? And when it landed, what then? What would it DO when it landed?

Then those huge wings started beating, slower and slower. The ground came nearer and nearer.

I looked down – and shivers went through me.

No. *No*.

What a sight. What a HORRIBLE sight.

A huge open space. Once, perhaps – a meadow, full of flowers, full of creatures...

But not now. Not *now*.

Now – a DUMP. A rotting, rusting dump. Stretching away in every direction.

A desolate place. Oozing and stinking. And *full* of old imms – huge old imms, industrial imms. Old imms heaped high on each other. Heaped high and abandoned. Left to rot. To rust. To ooze their poisons right into the ground.

This place, it must have had YEARS of dumping.

And I knew.

It was *here* that the creature would land.

It flung me from its claws and on to the ground. Then it towered above me.

Flames snaked out of its huge black nostrils. It arched its huge neck. Its vast snout opened wide – and a howl filled the air. A howl of FURY.

I crawled to my feet. My *wand*! I felt for my wand. Mervikk, Flibben – I could escape the same way. Disappear. Then I could run. Run and hide deep in that huge rotting dump. Hide somewhere it would NEVER find me.

But my wand – it was GONE. It must have fallen from my robe pocket, somewhere on that flight. Somewhere on this island... Quaking, trembling, I stared around. What could I do? Where could I go?

I was small, nimble. Could I scramble away? Run and hide in those imms? Dart and dodge, and make my way through? Make my escape?

No.

With one leap the creature could outrun me. With one roar it could send flames leaping around me. With one beat of its wings, it could grab me.

I *couldn't* escape. I could NOT escape.

Unless...

My Shudders… Could *they* help me now? Show me what to do?

They helped me with the ghouls. They helped me with the Haggfiend. Could they help me with this?

No.

My Shudders showed nothing that could help me. NOTHING.

Nothing but shadows and sounds. Nothing but flames and lights and explosions. Nothing but the running of feet and the flapping of wings and the howling of creatures…

Like this one.

Now the creature crouched. Hunched down on its huge legs. And howled, right in my face.

Rage blazed out from its glowing green eyes. Then it swiped at me with one huge webbed foot.

I stumbled. Fell back to the ground – and it hunched above me. Pinned me to the ground with one bony claw.

I could feel its breath. Hot smoky breath, smothering my face.

I could see right inside its huge snarling snout. See the tongue – big and black. See the teeth – HUGE jagged teeth – snapping in its jaw.

And I knew. It was over.

There was *nothing* I could do against this. Me, against this terrifying mutant.

With no Skritchetts. No wand. NOTHING to save me.

Except…

Except…

I did have one thing. Hooked right on to my belt…

The LANTERN. The lantern of the Valliants.

Chapter 38

I unhooked the lantern with trembling hands. Held it in front of me, and waved my hand.

The lantern grew bigger, the flame grew brighter. Bigger still, brighter still...

The creature snarled, then tossed its head. Uneasy, confused by the strong flaming light.

Then it backed away. Away from *me*...

Just a bit.

I jumped to my feet. Held the lantern in front of me.

The lantern grew bigger, the flame grew brighter. Ever bigger, ever brighter. Grew and grew into one huge flame of light. A huge *dazzling* flame of light. Light bright as the suns – streaming from the lantern.

Blazing straight at the eyes of that creature.

The creature *howled*. Then it staggered. It hunched. It clutched at its eyes with its huge webbed feet.

And now – the creature was *turning*. Away from the light – from that dazzling flame of light from the lantern...

Howling more and more and MORE. Its huge scaly head howling up at the sky.

And I stared.

At the creature, this huge hunched creature – who brought me here, to this place.

This creature – howling and howling. Howling right up at the vast empty sky.

And I knew.

Those howls – they were not howls of rage. Not howls of fury. Not even howls of pain at the light from the lantern.

Not now. Not any longer.

They were more... Something *more*.

Those howls – they were howls of *sorrow*. Howls of MISERY.

At what the creature was. At what it had become.

As if somehow, the creature *knew*. Somehow

sensed that THIS was the place. This was the cause of it all. Of it becoming the thing that it was…

The thing it had never EVER wanted to be.

And I stood there, holding the lantern of the Valliants. Watching the creature – this huge snarling monster – howling up at the sky. In sadness. In sorrow. In misery.

And I realised – this creature, this huge howling creature … it was a victim ITSELF.

Then, as I watched, as I listened, those howls began to die away. The rage, the fury – all gone. In its place, only sadness and sorrow and misery.

And the creature was starting to change. To shrink. To become – once more – the creature it TRULY wanted to be…

A small chirruppella, hopping at my feet.

★

I crouched down. Stared into the shining black eyes of the small chirruppella. And I knew. The battle with the creature, it was over.

But then, from deep inside the ground, from deep inside that vast dump of old abandoned imms – I heard a sound.

A rumbling and roaring sound. Like the roars of a huge angry beast. A beast in *terrible* TERRIBLE pain. A sound that grew louder and louder.

Then the ground beneath my feet began to shake. Tremors – vibrations – grew bigger, grew stronger, every second that passed.

And now that heap, that vast heap of old imms – it was shaking too.

I stared all around me. Terrified.

The island – something was happening to the ISLAND.

Chapter 39

I stood there, frozen. Something was changing. Something deep inside that oozing, poisoned ground.

I hooked the lantern – tiny once more – back to my belt, then ran. I ran, as fast as I could. Scrambled to get away from the dump. Up the path, towards higher ground. Up and up and up.

Then – below me, behind me – I heard a crunching, screeching, *earsplitting* sound.

I turned.

A magiquake… It was a MAGIQUAKE.

A crack – wide as a house – snaked its way through

the middle of the vast heap of old imms. A huge magiquake, ripping the poisoned ground apart. Carving and tearing its way through the dump.

And the imms went tumbling – imm after imm – into that jagged split in the ground. Huge imms smashing against each other, crushing each other as they tumbled downwards.

I clapped my hands to my ears. Tried to shut out the noise, the sounds – the *terrible* sounds…

Crunching sounds, screeching sounds. Crushing, grinding, roaring sounds. As every single imm on that vast rotting dump went tumbling down and was GONE. Swallowed up. Forever.

Then – that huge jagged split snapped shut.

But now, all around me, things were changing. The island *itself* – it was changing…

The trees – they were tearing their roots from the ground. Starting to sway, to stumble, to WALK. Staggering across the clearing, heaving themselves along – trees, maddened with rage. Stretching out branches like huge grasping fingers. Tree attacking tree. Branches whipping and tangling as they scratched and clawed at each other.

And the cliffs – they were starting to crumble. Cracks snaking through cliff after cliff. Boulders hurling themselves at each other. Smashing to pieces

as they collided. Even the water, the sea all around –
it was bubbling, and hissing, and boiling.

This island – it was raging with anger, with fury.
Poisoned. Tormented. Just like the creatures upon it.

And now the creatures of the island – they were
running. Fleeing. Stampeding past me.

Nothing angry, nothing raging, about these
creatures. They were TERRIFIED.

And so was I.

Because I knew those rumbling sounds, roaring
sounds… The pounding of paws, the squeals
and howls of terrified creatures… The lights, the
explosions, the flames.

These were the sounds from my Shudders. The
things that I had seen. And I knew, it was *this* – the
island ITSELF – that was the true danger…

✶

I ran. I ran and I ran. I ran upwards. Stumbling.
Dodging. Plants ripped themselves out of the ground
and slithered towards me. Curled themselves around
my legs, tried to trap me. Writhing things. Angry
things. *Terrifying* things.

"Mervikk!" I screamed. "MERVIKK! Where *are*
you?"

Whatever was happening, whatever this was – I
did NOT want to face it alone.

So I ran. Onwards and upwards. Searching and searching. Mervikk – where was he? *Where?*

Then I heard him. A voice, terrified. Calling out – again and again and again. "Flo! Flo! FLO!"

And there he was – running towards me, my wand in his hand. Flibben, ahead of him, snuffling at the ground. Seeking me out.

"What's HAPPENING?" Mervikk gasped.

"I don't know," I said. "I don't know."

And now, all around us, below us – all over the island – big bulging craters were bursting out of the ground. Like huge ugly pockmarks on the face of a terrible beast…

"What *are* they?" said Mervikk. "What?"

But I had no answer. They were like nothing I had seen before. Nothing I had read about. No magiographical thing I had EVER seen…

Big bulging craters spitting out vast flames. Spewing out green smoke. Big bursts of boiling green lava – *stinking* green lava – sliding over the sides, like poison. Smothering the ground all around them, the rampaging trees, the plants… Smothering everything.

A plant slithered – like a serpent – from the bushes right by me. A plant with a small hissing *mouth*. Sharp teeth gripped at my ankle. Tried to attack, to BITE.

I kicked the plant away. Just as, ahead, right beside Mervikk, the cliff crumbled away – and Mervikk disappeared over the edge.

✦

"MERVIKK!" I screamed. Then I threw myself to the ground and looked over the edge as, beside me, Flibben cheeped in terror.

Mervikk was far below us. On a ledge that was crumbling away. Faster and faster.

"Flo," he said, eyes wild with fear, arms reaching up. "*Help* me!"

"I *can't*," I said. "I can't reach."

I leaned out more. "Mervikk," I said. "Leviwitchery! You HAVE to do leviwitchery. NOW!"

Mervikk looked up at me. Mouth trembling. "I *can't*, Flo," he said. "I CAN'T!"

"Mervikk," I screamed. "You HAVE to! Think *light*! Think *strong*! Just like you did with Grandma. You can do it. You CAN!"

"Think light…" Mervikk said, his voice shaking. "Think *light*."

But nothing was happening. And now the ledge was starting to shake, to crumble right by Mervikk's left foot.

"*More*, Mervikk, MORE!" I screamed at him.

"Believe it, really *believe* you can do it! Remember, your dad – he NEEDS you! Think of your dad! Think LIGHT! Think STRONG! And *do* it. Do it NOW!"

Mervikk did.

He came soaring up, legs and arms flailing – and I grabbed him. Pulled him back on to the path.

A plant attacked. A *huge* plant – with FANGS. A hissing, spitting mouth and sharp fangs. A plant that twined and coiled its way around us. A plant that was too strong to break. Too strong to push off. A plant starting to pull tighter, then tighter still…

With a squawk of fury – Flibben leapt. He snapped and snapped with his big woddelflomp beak. Gnawing at the plant with his small sharp teeth.

The plant yowled in pain – then released us, and slithered away.

We ran again. Up and up. To the tallest cliff of all. To the cliff top facing straight towards the mainland. Straight towards Kronebay.

Then we huddled, backs against a rock. Stared around with terrified eyes.

There was nowhere to go. No way off this island.

And now the shaking was stronger. Much MUCH stronger. Every single one of those huge craters was shaking and shaking and shaking.

This whole island – shaking with rage, shaking with fury – it was about to destroy itself.

I sobbed. I just couldn't help it. I sank to the ground, and I sobbed. "Dad," I sobbed. "*Dad!* DAD! Where ARE you?"

And then Dad's words – the words he said that Witchen Day, the words he said as he showed me the lantern – started going round and round in my head.

Words so loud, so clear – it was as if Dad was standing right here. Right now. Here with me on this lonely, terrifying cliff top…

"…*for while there is one flicker of light in the lantern of the Valliants – then so must there be one flicker of hope in the heart of a Valliant.*"

A flicker of *light*… A flicker of *hope*…

HOPE.

Yes.

There *was* a flicker of light. There *was* a flicker of hope.

There WAS.

I was *not* giving up. Not yet.

Mum, Hetty, Grandma. I would see them again.
I *would*.

And Dad…

Dad too.

Yes. Skritchetts – we *would* all be together again.
We WOULD.

And I jumped to my feet, and unhooked the
lantern, then waved my hand. And I stood. As *tall* as
I could. Then I held up the lantern – the lantern of
the Valliants…

"Forever light, forever hope!" I shouted. "*Forever
light, forever hope!* FOREVER LIGHT, FOREVER
HOPE!"

And light from the flame went soaring. Dazzling
bright light, streaming from the lantern of the
Valliants. Streaming and streaming across the
darkening sky.

And then I saw wings.

Huge wings.

Wings, beating and beating and beating. Beating
straight towards us.

Wings, guided by the light streaming from the
lantern of the Valliants…

The huge white wings of a UNICORN.

Chapter 40

I was *trembling*. Trembling from head to foot.

Trembling, as that huge white unicorn swirled down from the sky. Swirled nearer and nearer and nearer.

Because I knew, just *knew*.

It was DAD.

And now – me, Mervikk, we would be *safe*. Dad would keep us safe. Safe, from whatever was happening to the island.

So the craters blazing... The ground shaking...

None of it mattered. NONE of it. Not now. Not this second.

Because this second – *nothing* in the world mattered as much as this.

THIS.

The sight of those huge unicorn wings, beating nearer and nearer.

Then – at last – the unicorn was here. *Here.*

Landing on four huge unicorn hooves. Landing right beside me. Staring down at me, with its huge wise eyes. With its vast white wings. With its flowing white mane.

And then – the unicorn was gone. And a witchman stood there.

A *witchman*…

I stared. I stared and stared and *stared* at the witchman.

A TALL witchman…

A witchman with no cape, no mask…

And the witchman stared back at me. Stared and stared, a look of wonder – of joy – on his face.

Feelings flooded through me. Flooded through me like a river bursting its banks. Feelings so big, so happy I could hardly *breathe*.

And I knew that – right now, right here, right this moment – I was the happiest witchkid in the *whole* of Witchworld. The happiest witchkid EVER.

Then the witchman spoke – in a voice I knew so

well. So SO well…

"Flo," he said, and I could hear his voice cracking. "Florence Klarity Skritchett…"

"Dad," I said. "*Dad!* DAD!"

Then I hurled myself at him.

Because Dad – he was here. Here, at last.

Dad, *my* dad – he was BACK.

Part
Five

Chapter 41

Me and Mervikk – we watched every last moment of that island. Of that poisoned, dying island.

We watched from high in the sky. Both of us, clinging to the back of the huge hovering unicorn, Flibben tucked tightly between us…

Watched as surging green lava roared across the island. Engulfed every tree, every cliff, every single thing on it.

And then – with a roar, a vast bellowing ROAR – the island *exploded*. Exploded in a shower of sparks and flames. Of searing flashes of light that lit up the sky.

And was gone.

Swallowed up by the vast ocean around it.

FOREVER.

Then – with one beat of those huge white wings – the unicorn turned. Flew mile after mile, through the vast night sky. Flew on and on over the wide dark sea, until – ahead, in the distance, were the lights of Kronebay.

And, shining out, from high on a cliff top – were the lights of Vistarikka Villa. Growing nearer and nearer and nearer.

Then the unicorn landed. Softly, gently, at the bottom of the garden. And me and Mervikk tumbled to the ground.

Home… Safe… At *last*.

✦

I went running, Mervikk beside me. Running as fast as I could, up to the house.

It was Dad's idea.

"Not too many shocks at once," he said to me, grinning. "First – let your mother know you're both back, safe and well."

So we left Dad there, at the bottom of the garden. A unicorn once more. A pale silhouette against the big night sky – now lit by the twinkling of millions of stars.

And we ran. Up the garden, towards the terrace. Towards the house.

Then we heard shrieks. Loud shrieks from inside, and feet pounding. And here they came. Mum, Hetty — both hurtling out on to the terrace. Both palest green. Both charging towards us, down the steps to the lawn.

"Flo, Mervikk!" Mum shrieked. "Where have you *been*? Where have you BEEN! Witchwardens are out all over Kronebay, looking for you! Alerts are in place all over the Witchenlands!"

Then Mum hugged me — so tight I could hardly breathe. "Flo," she said. "I thought I'd LOST you!"

She hugged me again. "But I haven't. I haven't!" she said. "My strange little Skritchett — you're *back*!"

Then Hetty pushed her out of the way. "My turn," she said. "MY turn." And she hugged me just as tight — and started *wailing*. Wailing right in my EAR.

"Flo, worry is not GOOD for a witchteen!" Hetty wailed. "Worry can cause *wrinkles*! And I *was* worried, Flo — so SO worried! Do you have ANY idea of the worry you caused me?"

Then the wailing stopped — just like that. And Hetty grabbed me by the shoulders. Stared at me sternly. "So," she said, snapping her fingers.

"Witchteen needing INFO, Flo. Where were you? *Where?*"

Now Hetty started wagging a finger at me. "And wherever you went, whatever your story," she said, "it had better be good."

"Hetty," I said, and I felt a smile creep right across my face. "It *is* good. Trust me, it IS."

Now Mum had moved on to Mervikk. "And Mervikk," she said, hugging him tight. "Mervikk – you're *safe*. You're SAFE!"

"Only just, Flo's-mum," beamed Mervikk. "Me and Flo – we watched an island EXPLODE! One of the Wild Isles!"

"Wow," said Hetty, eyes popping. "*Wow!*"

Mum looked utterly baffled. "You watched an island EXPLODE? A *Wild Isle*?" she said.

"Yes," Mervikk said. "Whoosh. The whole thing went up. There were big flames and lava – stinking oozing lava – and then it was GONE!"

Then he beamed more. "Me and Flo were VERY lucky to escape," he said. "Because we were actually *stuck* on that exploding island."

Mum went the palest green I have *ever* seen her. She clutched on to a garden chair. "Lucky to ESCAPE?" she said, in a small wobbling voice. "STUCK on that island?"

"Yes, Flo's-mum," beamed Mervikk. "But it was all right. The unicorn saved us – JUST in time."

Mum looked VERY wobbly now. She stared down the garden, at the unicorn. A huge pale shadow in the light from the stars.

"The unicorn," she said, faintly, rubbing her head. "The unicorn…"

"Mum," said Hetty, butting in. "We should THANK the unicorn. It's only *polite*. Thank it for saving your younger daughter. And a witchchild in our care."

"Yes," said Mum, even more faintly. "We should… We should *thank* the unicorn."

"Sugar lumps," said Hetty confidently. "We'll give it sugar lumps."

Mum nodded. "Here boy," she said – a little nervously, beckoning with her hand. "Here boy."

The unicorn came trotting up the garden. Then, just as Hetty turned, ready to fetch some sugar lumps – Mum shrieked.

She started to wobble, to sway…

Because the unicorn was gone. And there, standing in front of her – was Dad.

"You… You…" said Mum faintly. Then her legs began to crumple.

"Oops," said Dad – catching her as she fell. Then

he propped her up in the garden chair. And stared down at her with a smile on his face.

"Kristabel Skritchett," he said, smiling more. "I do believe you are swooning. Actually SWOONING."

"I… You…" Mum said.

"Sit," Dad said. "And breathe. Long, slow breaths."

And Mum *did* sit. Staring and staring. Breathing … just about.

As for Hetty – she was stuck to the spot. Standing, still as a statue. Mouth hanging right open.

Then she took one step – one VERY wobbly step – towards Dad. Then another, and another. Went up close to him, as close as she could – and *peered*.

"Dad…?" she whispered. "Dad…? DAD…?"

Then she started jumping up and down. "Dad!" she shrieked. "*Dad!* DAD! You ARE Dad! You're *Dad!*"

"Hetty," Dad said, with a laugh in his voice. "Henrietta Velocity Skritchett – I am indeed Dad!" Then he scooped her up, and twirled her round and round and round.

"Dizzy," Hetty shrieked, in the end. "Witchteen DIZZY. *Stop* now!"

And Dad did. He put her down. Peered closely at her…

At her *nose*.

Hetty gasped. Turned sideways. Grabbed his arm. "Do you see it, Dad?" she said. "Do you SEE it, Dad? *Do* you? DO you?"

"Hetty," Dad said – and now his smile stretched right across his face. "I do."

And that was when we heard a cackle – from high up in the sky. A loud cackle of laughter. "I *knew* it!" shouted a triumphant voice. "I KNEW it!"

We looked up. And there she was.

An old witch riding a broomstick. An old witch dressed in long black robes, black as black. An old witch wearing a big pointy hat with stars all over it…

Grandma.

"Lyle Skritchett!" she cackled. "I *knew* you'd be back! I KNEW it!"

And – just as she landed – the bells of Kronebay rang out.

One… Two… Three… Twelve times.

It was midnight.

Midnight.

And today – it was WITCHEN DAY.

Chapter 42

Dad had NO memory – none at all. No memory of his struggle with that huge ghoul, up at the Ice Volcano.

And, for a very long time, no memory of his life before. No clue to who he was, where he lived, his life as a witchman.

Just one thing he *did* remember. The spellstick in his pocket – what it was, how to use it.

But beyond that, nothing. Nothing before waking in a snow-troll cave. Injured – but with a new magiskill…

Semblawitchery.

"They talked of finding me, Flo, deep in a snow drift," Dad told me. "Of digging me out, of carrying me to their cave. And they cared for me like one of their own – they were the kindest of creatures."

Then Dad's face darkened. "I learnt so much from those snow trolls," he said, "of their thoughts and their ways. But I learnt other things too. BAD things. Bad things about witches. They told me of hunters, who would strike in the depths of winter. Trap the snow trolls. Then steal their thick winter fur. Leave them to shiver and to freeze."

Now Dad's eyes were gleaming. "But *not* that winter, Flo," he said. "For that winter, when the hunters came – tiptoeing through the forest, in search of snow trolls – I was ready. And I struck! Did a robe-ridding spell, then a blizzard spell. Then left those hunters, shivering in their underpants. Shivering – just as the snow trolls did!"

And Dad heard more. From gritterbacks, who told him how poachers would slice off their antlers. How gritterbacks with no antlers struggle to balance while their two heads feed. Growing weaker and weaker, with each passing day.

"The snow trolls, the gritterbacks…" said Dad. "I was *ashamed*. I wanted NO part of that world of witches. And so, with no identity of my own – I

CREATED an identity, a disguise!"

And so, disguised in the cape, and the mask – he struck once again. Did a magicreation, locked the poachers in cages for one whole day and night. With a banquet – a vast marble table, groaning with dishes – just beyond their reach.

"I realised," said Dad, "THIS, then, was my skill. To listen to the creatures of Witchenwild, to hear of the ways witches mistreated them. And to *act*. To make witches *think*."

Dad smiled at me. "And so, Flo," he said, "time went by up there in Witchenwild. Days, weeks, months, *years* – I had no idea. But then, one rainy day, something happened… A tune came into my head. A *very* special tune."

And I knew what Dad meant. Dad and my tune. The tune we made up that rainy day – so SO long ago.

"That tune, Flo," Dad said, "it changed things. Filled me with sadness. With a sense of things missing. With a yearning, a longing for something – but I didn't know what. And now, for the very first time – I *wanted* to remember. Who I was. Where I came from."

And so the day came when Dad left the snow trolls, heading south.

"Something was calling me," Dad said. "Small flashes of memory – just beyond my grasp. Faint glimpses of a life I once had. Calling me south. Always south."

South…

Where he met trolls – the forest trolls, who told of their suffering, of pain, in the pipes of the Potions2Go factory.

And unicorns…

"Unicorns, Flo," Dad said, "those wisest of creatures. The kings of the skies. They told of the dark deeds of that witchman. Of the Wild Isles in danger, in pain. Of seariders, laden with cargo, travelling to the Shimmering. So I followed – but then came the fog, sent to swirl around me while they made their escape. So, disguised as the guard boggle – I pounced on the map. And set out for the island."

The island…

Where I was waiting. Waiting with the lantern to warn him.

"I puzzled and puzzled," Dad said. "Those flashes of light, that code warning of danger – how did I know it? And the lantern – who was it who held it? Then, back in that villa, disguised as the tiniest of scuttlepins, I heard terrible things."

And once more, Dad's face grew dark and grave. "They spoke of witchchildren, abandoned, alone on the island. And of the lantern – and the witchchild who held it… Florence Skritchett!"

Dad shivered. "And *that*, Flo, hearing your name – THAT was the moment," he said. "My first true memory returned. Of Witchen Day, of handing you the parcel. Of the lantern – the lantern of the Valliants. And I flew, Flo. I flew on wings of *terror*. Flew with no thought in my head but you… You, Florence Skritchett – in DANGER!"

Dad was headlines, of course…

LYLE SKRITCHETT REUNITED WITH FAMILY!
MASKED SEMBLAWITCH IS LYLE SKRITCHETT!

And I was too…

STOWAWAY FLO IN MUTANT MAYHEM!

I told Dad of my time on the island – me and Mervikk alone with that huge mutant dragon. How flames of fire leapt into the cave where we huddled.

How it clutched me in those huge clawed feet, as it flew far above the island. How the plants grabbed, and the trees fought, and the poisonous green lava swallowed the ground all around us…

And Dad went pale as he listened.

Then I told him of my battle with the Haggfiend. Of clinging on to that vast stone statue, as the huge hairy Haggfiend came leaping and hissing, green flames flickering in her furious eyes…

And Dad went even paler.

Then he hugged me tight. "Florence Skritchett," he said. "You are INDEED the Eighth Wonder of Witchworld!"

"The *Ninth*, Dad," I said, and told him of the ghouls, the Eighth Wonder of Witchworld – the Ice Statues of the Frozen Wastes.

I told him how Skritchetts saved Witchworld from ghouls. And of the rogue ghoul – the worst ghoul of all. How it towered above me, baring its teeth, stretching out its claws, its terrible claws…

And Dad went SO pale I thought he might faint. "Flo, stop, STOP!" he said, with his hands to his ears. "You're *scaring* me. Do you have any GOOD news to tell?"

"Oh yes, Dad," I said. "Plenty!"

So I told him all my good news. Every bit I could think of.

That I can now ride a broomstick, and that I've got my own wand. That I did Force 7 fumawitchery on my very first go. That I know lots of words in Fangwegian, including the ones for toenails and warts and whiskers. That I've seen forest pixies up close – so close I could touch them. And that I have a very good friend, who is a small urban troll…

So SO much news.

And – at last – Dad was *here*. Here to TELL.

As for that Wild Isle, me and Mervikk spent a long time telling witchwardens about it. And Mr Potions2Go and Grimmelda Hurlstruk are in big, BIG trouble.

But they've both disappeared, so they're headlines too…

POTIONS MOGUL AND DAUGHTER ON THE RUN!

And there were MORE headlines…

TRASHTAX SCANDAL INVOLVES GOVERNMENT MINISTERS!

Dad explained it to me. How all three Witchglobe Wellbeing Witchministers from the last twelve years are in disgrace. For arranging to turn off the Shimmering – then, in return, having long holidays at Mr Potions2Go's big houses, all for free.

And one of those witchministers is in the biggest disgrace – the one who started the arrangement, twelve years back…

Ariadne Von Trinkpott.

Grandma snorted when she heard the name. Because Grandma does NOT like Ariadne Von Trinkpott. Not since she found out that Ariadne was lying to the government, and claiming money she shouldn't.

"That witch is a crook!" Grandma said. "A crook as Welfare Witchminister and a crook as Witchglobe Wellbeing Witchminister!"

Talking of Grandma she has – *finally* – told me how Great-Grandma got the Shudders…

It was all because Great-Grandma was BORED. Life was dull back then for rich witchgirls like her. They were supposed to sit around, practising tidying up spells and flower arranging spells – waiting to grow up and find a rich witchboy to marry.

But not Great-Grandma. Oh no.

She used to sneak out at night on her broomstick – from aged only *nine* – and go exploring deep in the forest. Then one night she found a cave, the secret potions workshop of Jeraboam Inkbold – the only witchman to get rid of the problem of Stink in truth potion, the Stink that means no witch is ever fooled into drinking it.

Jeraboam tried to sneak his truth potion into the food at a big important banquet so the government, who'd been telling lies about the First Wand War – saying it was going well when it wasn't – would start telling the truth.

But then he got caught – and smashed the bottle of truth potion, refusing to say how he made it. So they chucked him in the Roaring River for treason.

Which meant his secret workshop was abandoned, all covered in cobwebs and dust – until Great-Grandma found it.

She started running around, opening bottles and jars, chucking things into a cauldron. Then she bubbled up the mixture. And drank it.

Which was FOOLHARDY, I think you'll agree, as potions are dangerous things. But nothing happened to Great-Grandma. Just a few strange flutterings under her corset…

Until, that is, she went to Drool – and had her

very first Shudder. Glimpses of the deadly dodger attack.

"By one chance in billions," Grandma told me proudly, "Mummy combined her stolen ingredients in perfect quantities – and invented a Shuddering potion. A way to see the TRUTH of witchhistory!"

Grandma has had a proposal. A marriage proposal from Gilbert. He even got down on one knee to do it.

Grandma just patted him on the hand, and helped him back up to his feet. "Gilbert," she said. "I am most flattered. But really, we are NOT suited. You're far too stubborn – and so am I. Besides, I already have a MUCH BETTER match in mind for you."

So Gilbert's going on a blind date next week…

With Lily's great-aunt, Auntie Mims.

Talking of dates – even though Hetty sent Errken *seven* Kwikpiks of her and Archie on their date at the witchfliks, it failed.

"Flo," said Hetty. "Errken is *still* with Veracity, and I have decided – he has had his chance. It is time to MOVE ON."

Then she nodded. "And I," she said proudly, "am going to FIND myself."

"Find yourself?" I said, confused.

"Find out who I REALLY am," Hetty said, nodding. "By joining TeenTrekkers. Archie is being a TeenTrekker this summer – and so am I."

"Archie? You're going with Archie?" I said, even more confused.

"Among others, Flo," said Hetty. "Four weeks living in tents. No skychatters, no witchfixers. None of the frills and frivolities of life as a witchteen. Just nature, fresh air, and long, LONG treks every day. Up mountains, down ravines. Crossing rivers by raft. Dodging snippersnappers in creeks. Finding our way by the suns and the stars. Learning to fish, and to hunt – to live off only what we find on the land."

She wagged her finger at me. "Because, Flo," she said, "before I find a boyfriend – I must find *myself*. Find out who I really AM. My strengths. My weaknesses. My hopes. My fears. Only *then* can a relationship truly work."

She sat there, looking very earnest…

Too earnest.

"Hetty," I said – and I felt my eyes narrowing, "are you *lying*?"

Hetty threw back her head and cackled and cackled. "TOTALLY lying," she beamed.

Then she leaned forward and patted my hand, eyes shining. "Flo," she said. "Do you *know* how many witchboys go on TeenTrekkers? *Ten* witchboys to every *three* witchgirls. TEN!"

✴

As for Mum – she's been headline news herself…

HOCUS POCUS BOSS TO LEAD I CARE! CAMPAIGN!

She had a long lunch with the boss of *Scoop!*, and a long talk. And it turned out they were both bored with being the boss of their magazines.

So, by the end of their lunch, they had decided three things.

First, that they were going to start a NEW magazine. Together. One with more important stuff in it. And that they would call the new magazine *Witchweek*.

Second, that the **I CARE!** campaign needed to carry on and get bigger. Get *more* witchkid carers the breaks they deserved. And that to do that, it needed a powerful boss – one who could nag the government and get things done…

Mum.

And third, that the very first issue of *Witchweek*

should feature a witchkid carer on the cover…

Mervikk.

Mum and Mervikk even did an interview on *Haggnews*. And the new Welfare Witchminister – one Grandma approves of – was watching it. She ordered a government review of witchkid carers to start right away.

And Mervikk got his own headlines…

WITCHKID CARER DISCOVERS CURE FOR STUMBLES!

Because that night, as Mervikk combed out all the knots in Flibben's tufty hair, feeling upset that the island was gone, and along with it, all the grimbleshank plants – he made a discovery.

Ten little seeds caught up in Flibben's hair…

Seeds of the grimbleshank plant.

Gilbert tested them all – and one seed seemed odd, possibly mutant. Which means witchboffins may find out useful things about mutants from it.

But, more importantly, the other seeds are busy growing.

It will be less than three months, Gilbert reckons, before the cure for Stumbles is ready.

Mervikk was thrilled. About the cure – and about the headlines.

"Me," he beamed. "A *discoverer!* DISCOVERER of the cure for Stumbles! Discoverer of the grimbleshank seeds! Discoverer of the mutant fairy! Who knows what I might discover next!"

✳

And as for that Witchen Day – it was the best one EVER.

Skritchetts all together, all celebrating. And Mervikk and Gilbert, both there, joining in.

All of us, standing round the Witchen tree. Smelling that Witchen-tree smell. Hearing a knock on the front door – witches, singing Witchen Day songs, collecting for homeless goblins.

Then – the presents, and the Witchen Day meal. The big table. The flickering candles. All of us, wearing silly hats, pulling crackers, blowing whistles.

And afterwards, playing games. Rug racing – crouched down on rugs, flying up and down the garden, as fast as we could. Playing magiquestions – shouting our questions at Mum, all trying to guess her magicreations before she finished them.

Then me and Mervikk, huddled together, doing a one-thousand-piece forest pixie jigsaw – my present from Grandma. Hetty, modelling her new earrings and trying out shrinking spells with her new spellstick. Grandma, testing her X-ray specs – a present from Gilbert – on Mum.

And Dad...

I kept having to pinch myself. REALLY pinch myself. Just to check that this wasn't a dream. That this was actually real.

That Dad was here.

Here.

Doing silly Dad things. Joining in loudly with the Witchen Day singers. Laughing so hard when his cracker fairy read out its joke that he fell off his chair.

And opening his presents. The presents we had saved, all this time. Hoping and hoping that – one day – Dad would be back to open them.

And he was. He *was*.

Dad was HERE.

And late that evening – me and Hetty saw them...

Mum and Dad. Standing out on the terrace. Talking and talking and talking.

Hetty clasped her hands. She looked at me, eyes shining. "Flo," she said. "This could be it... Mum... Dad... Back together – an actual HAPPY ending!"

And I stood there, thinking. Then I turned to Hetty.

"Hetty," I said. "Mum… Dad… I don't know what will happen. But I *do* know this. That, right here, right now – Dad is *back*. And here we all are, us Skritchetts, together again. Together for Witchen Day."

Then I felt a great big smile spread right across my face. "And THAT," I said, giving Hetty a hug, "is ALL the happy ending I need!"

And it was. It really, REALLY was.